D1269154

Sir Arthur Conan Doyle's
The Adventure of the Engineer's Thumb

Adapted by: Vincent Goodwin

Illustrated by: Ben Dunn

magic
wagon

visit us at
www.abdopublishing.com

Published by Magic Wagon, a division of the ABDO Group, PO Box 398166, Minneapolis, MN, 55439.

Printed in the United States of America, North Mankato, Minnesota.
022012
092012
This book contains at least 10% recycled materials.

Written by Sir Arthur Conan Doyle
Adapted by Vincent Goodwin
Illustrated by Ben Dunn
Colored by Robby Bevard
Lettered by Doug Dlin
Edited by Stephanie Hedlund and Rochelle Baltzer
Interior layout by Antarctic Press
Cover art by Ben Dunn
Cover design by Abbey Fitzgerald

Library of Congress Cataloging-in-Publication Data

Goodwin, Vincent.
Sir Arthur Conan Doyle's The adventure of the engineer's thumb / adapted by Vincent Goodwin ; illustrated by Ben Dunn.
p. cm. -- (The graphic novel adventures of Sherlock Holmes)
Summary: Retold in graphic novel form, a hydraulic engineer's loss of a thumb leads Sherlock Holmes to a band of criminals.
ISBN 978-1-61641-893-9
1. Doyle, Arthur Conan, Sir, 1859-1930. Adventure of the engineer's thumb--Adaptations. 2. Holmes, Sherlock (Fictitious character)--Comic books, strips, etc. 3. Holmes, Sherlock (Fictitious character)--Juvenile fiction. 4. Graphic novels. [1. Graphic novels. 2. Doyle, Arthur Conan, Sir, 1859-1930. Adventure of the engineer's thumb--Adaptations. 3. Mystery and detective stories.] I. Dunn, Ben, ill. II. Doyle, Arthur Conan, Sir, 1859-1930. Adventure of the engineer's thumb. III. Title. IV. Title: Adventure of the engineer's thumb. V. Series: Goodwin, Vincent. Graphic novel adventures of Sherlock Holmes.
PZ7.7.G66Sig 2012
741.5'973--dc23

2011052260

Table of Contents

Cast

Sherlock Holmes

Dr. John Watson

Mr. Victor Hatherly

Colonel Lysander Stark, AKA Fritz

Mystery Woman

Dr. Becher, AKA Mr. Ferguson

Inspector Bradstreet

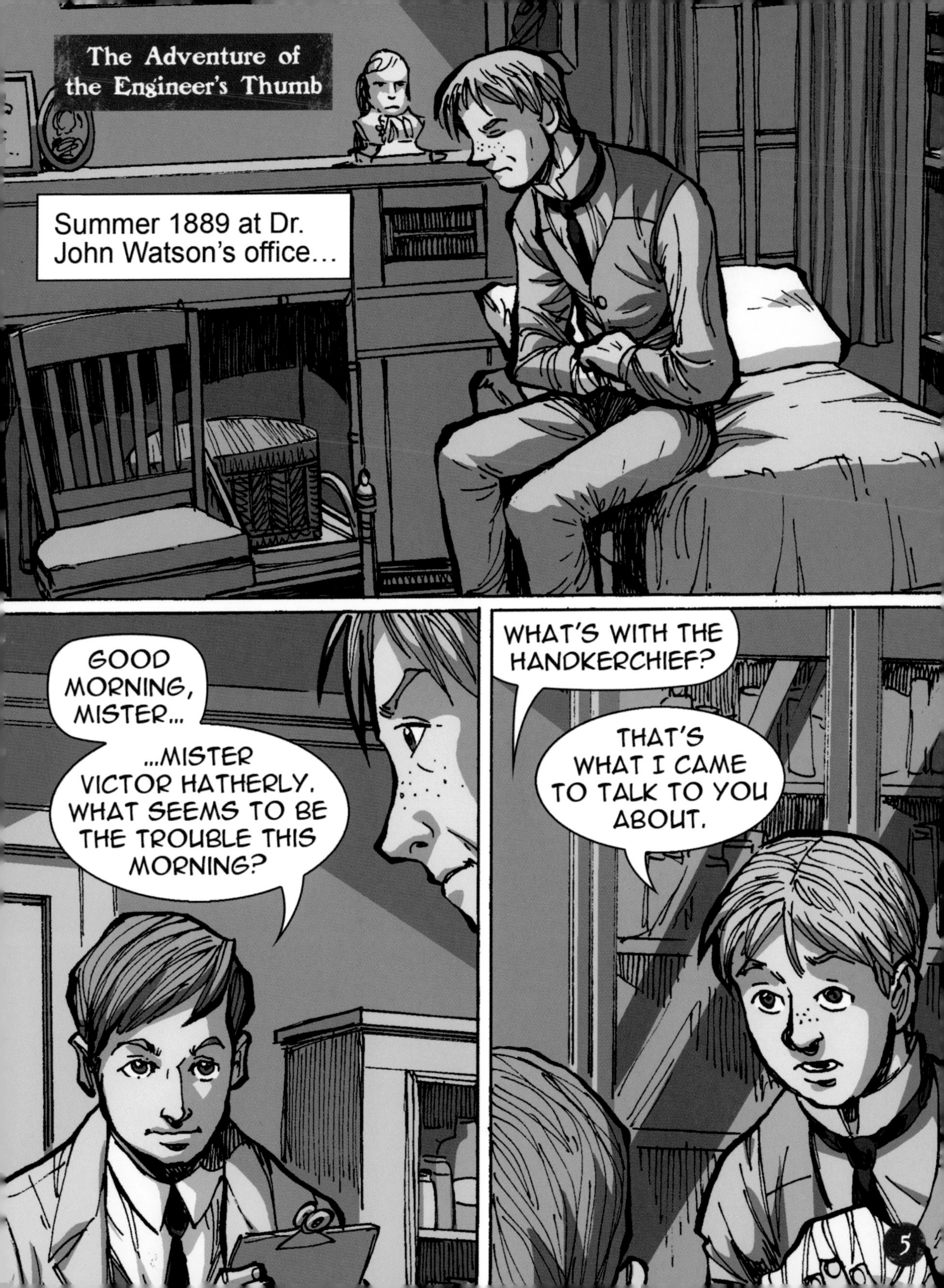
The Adventure of the Engineer's Thumb
Summer 1889 at Dr. John Watson's office…
GOOD MORNING, MISTER...
...MISTER VICTOR HATHERLY. WHAT SEEMS TO BE THE TROUBLE THIS MORNING?
WHAT'S WITH THE HANDKERCHIEF?
THAT'S WHAT I CAME TO TALK TO YOU ABOUT.

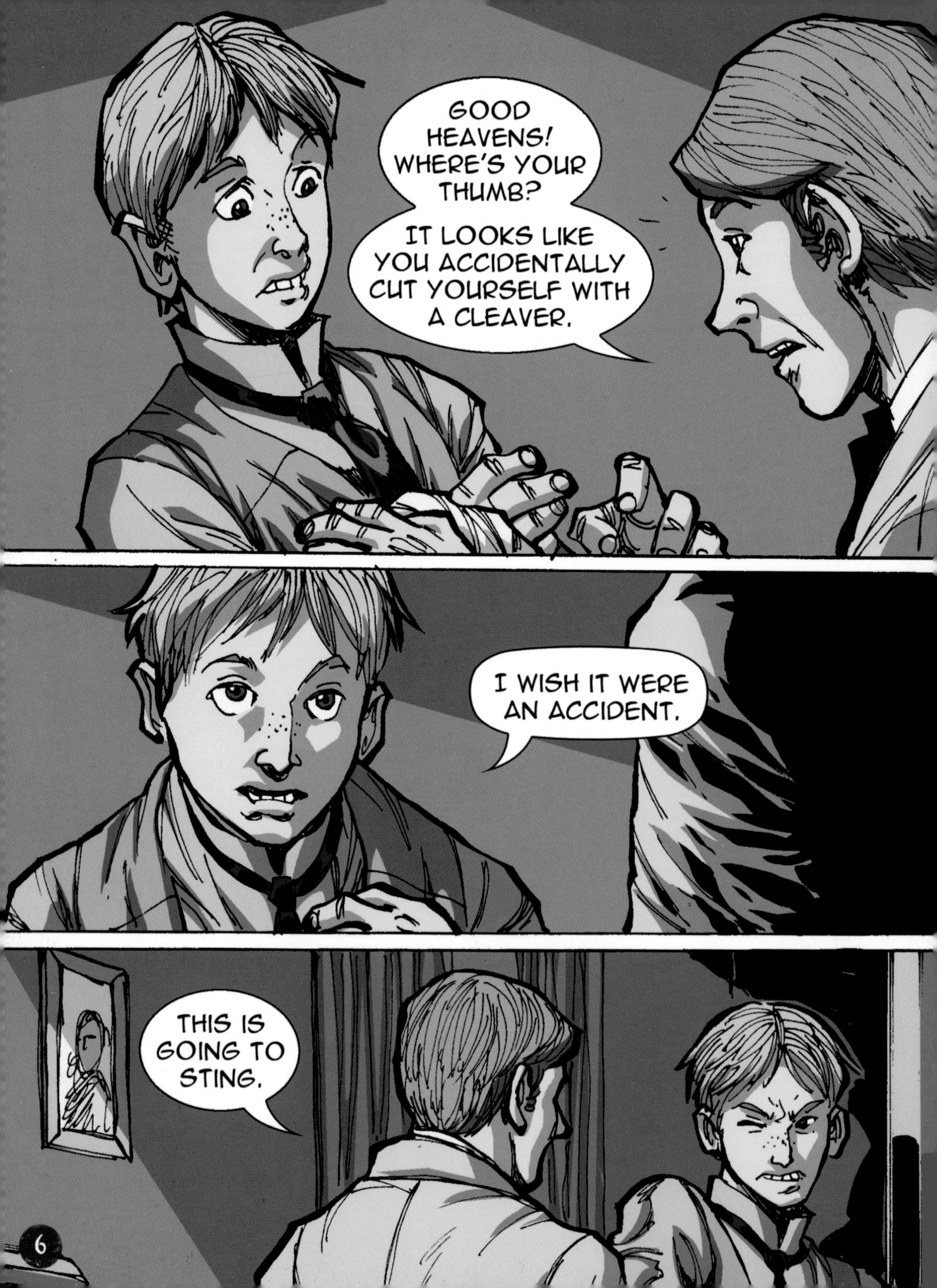
GOOD HEAVENS! WHERE'S YOUR THUMB?
IT LOOKS LIKE YOU ACCIDENTALLY CUT YOURSELF WITH A CLEAVER.
I WISH IT WERE AN ACCIDENT.
THIS IS GOING TO STING.

IF SOMEONE TRIED TO HURT YOU, YOU SHOULD GO TO THE POLICE.

THAT'S THE THING. I DON'T KNOW WHO ATTACKED ME.

JUST BETWEEN US, IF I WASN'T MISSING MY THUMB, I'D BE SURPRISED IF THEY'D BELIEVE MY STORY. I DON'T HAVE PROOF TO BACK IT UP.

THEN I STRONGLY URGE YOU TO VISIT MR. SHERLOCK HOLMES. HE HAS A WAY OF SOLVING UNSOLVABLE MYSTERIES.

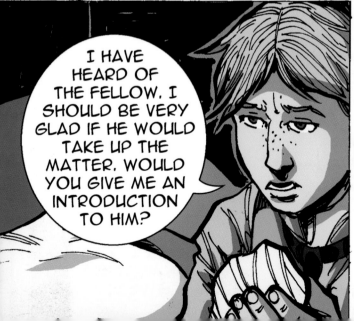

I HAVE HEARD OF THE FELLOW. I SHOULD BE VERY GLAD IF HE WOULD TAKE UP THE MATTER. WOULD YOU GIVE ME AN INTRODUCTION TO HIM?

I'LL DO BETTER. I'LL TAKE YOU ROUND TO HIM MYSELF.

DR. J. WATSON M.D.

7

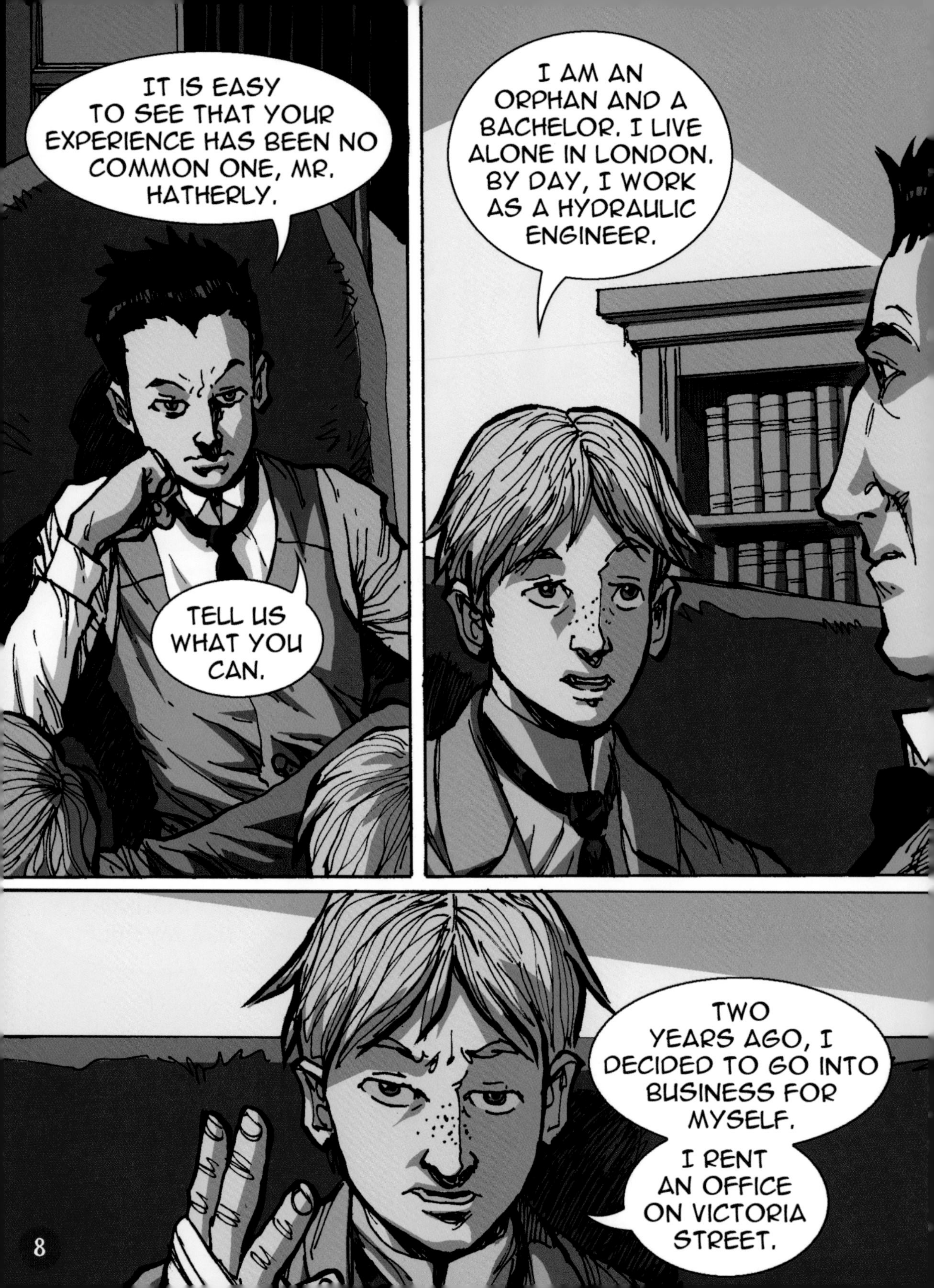

IT IS EASY TO SEE THAT YOUR EXPERIENCE HAS BEEN NO COMMON ONE, MR. HATHERLY.
TELL US WHAT YOU CAN.
I AM AN ORPHAN AND A BACHELOR. I LIVE ALONE IN LONDON. BY DAY, I WORK AS A HYDRAULIC ENGINEER.
TWO YEARS AGO, I DECIDED TO GO INTO BUSINESS FOR MYSELF.
I RENT AN OFFICE ON VICTORIA STREET.

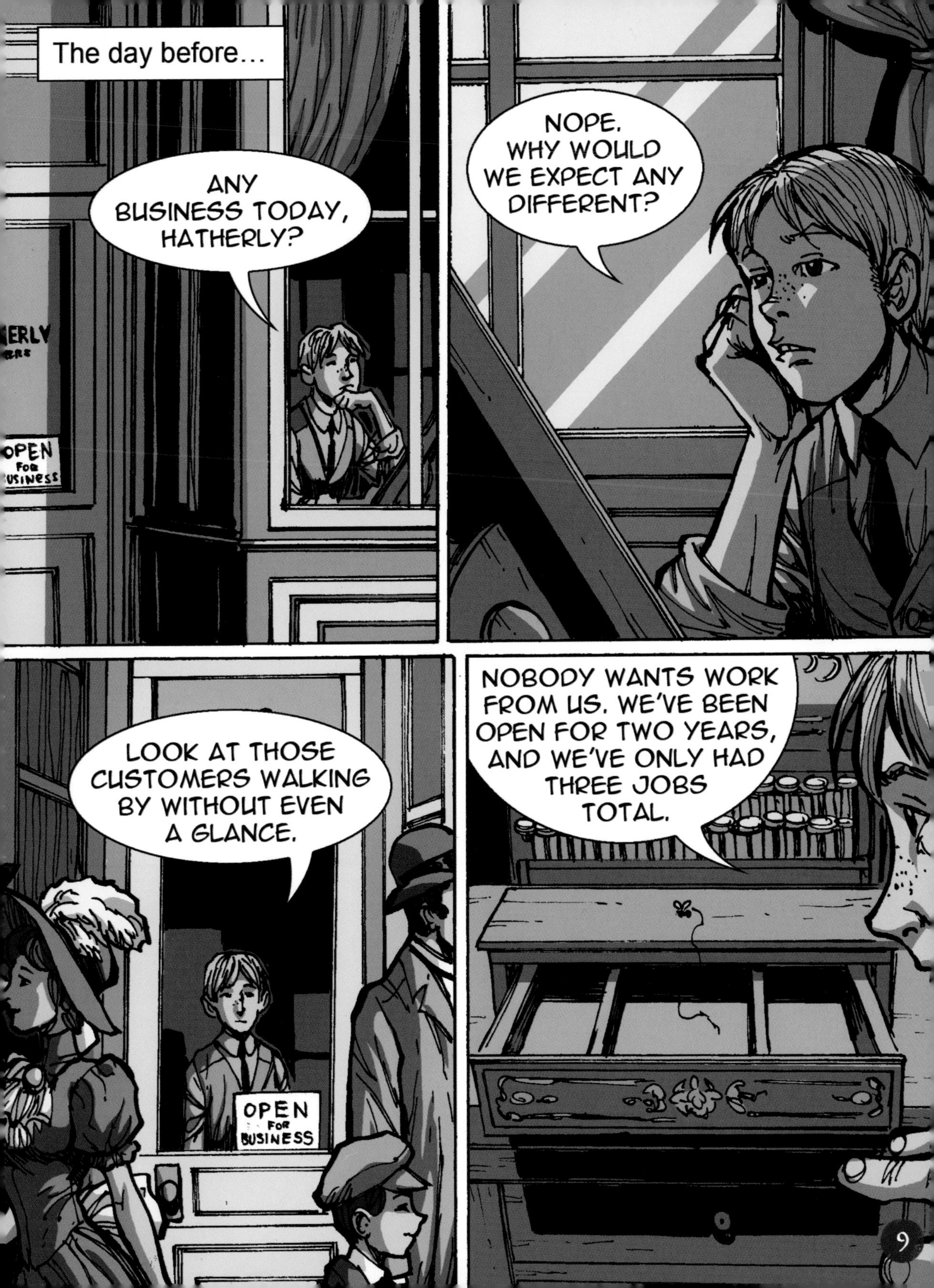
The day before…
ERLY
OPEN FOR USINESS
ANY BUSINESS TODAY, HATHERLY?
NOPE. WHY WOULD WE EXPECT ANY DIFFERENT?
LOOK AT THOSE CUSTOMERS WALKING BY WITHOUT EVEN A GLANCE.
OPEN FOR BUSINESS
NOBODY WANTS WORK FROM US. WE'VE BEEN OPEN FOR TWO YEARS, AND WE'VE ONLY HAD THREE JOBS TOTAL.

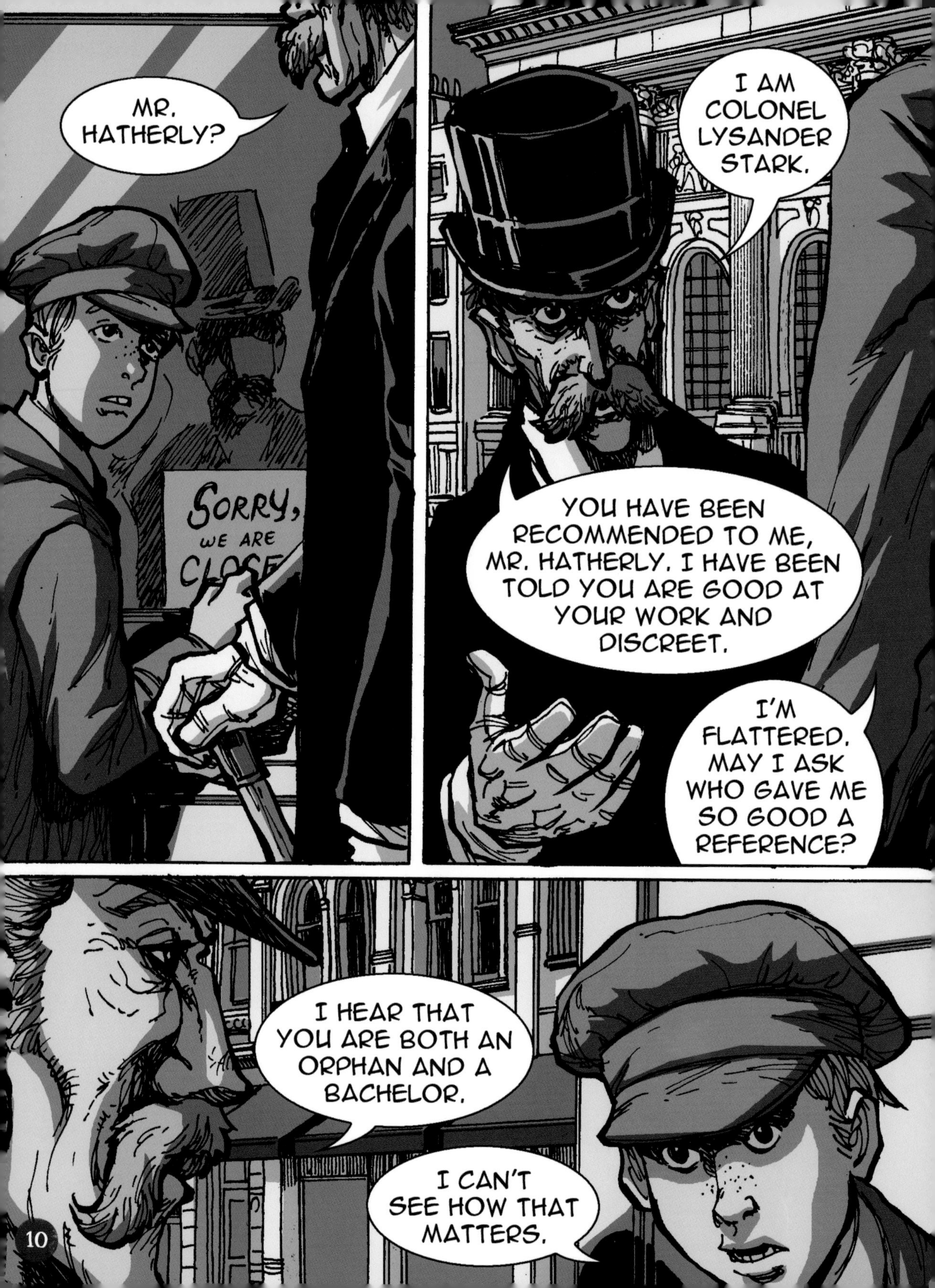
MR. HATHERLY?
SORRY, WE ARE CLOSE
I AM COLONEL LYSANDER STARK.
YOU HAVE BEEN RECOMMENDED TO ME, MR. HATHERLY. I HAVE BEEN TOLD YOU ARE GOOD AT YOUR WORK AND DISCREET.
I'M FLATTERED. MAY I ASK WHO GAVE ME SO GOOD A REFERENCE?
I HEAR THAT YOU ARE BOTH AN ORPHAN AND A BACHELOR.
I CAN'T SEE HOW THAT MATTERS.

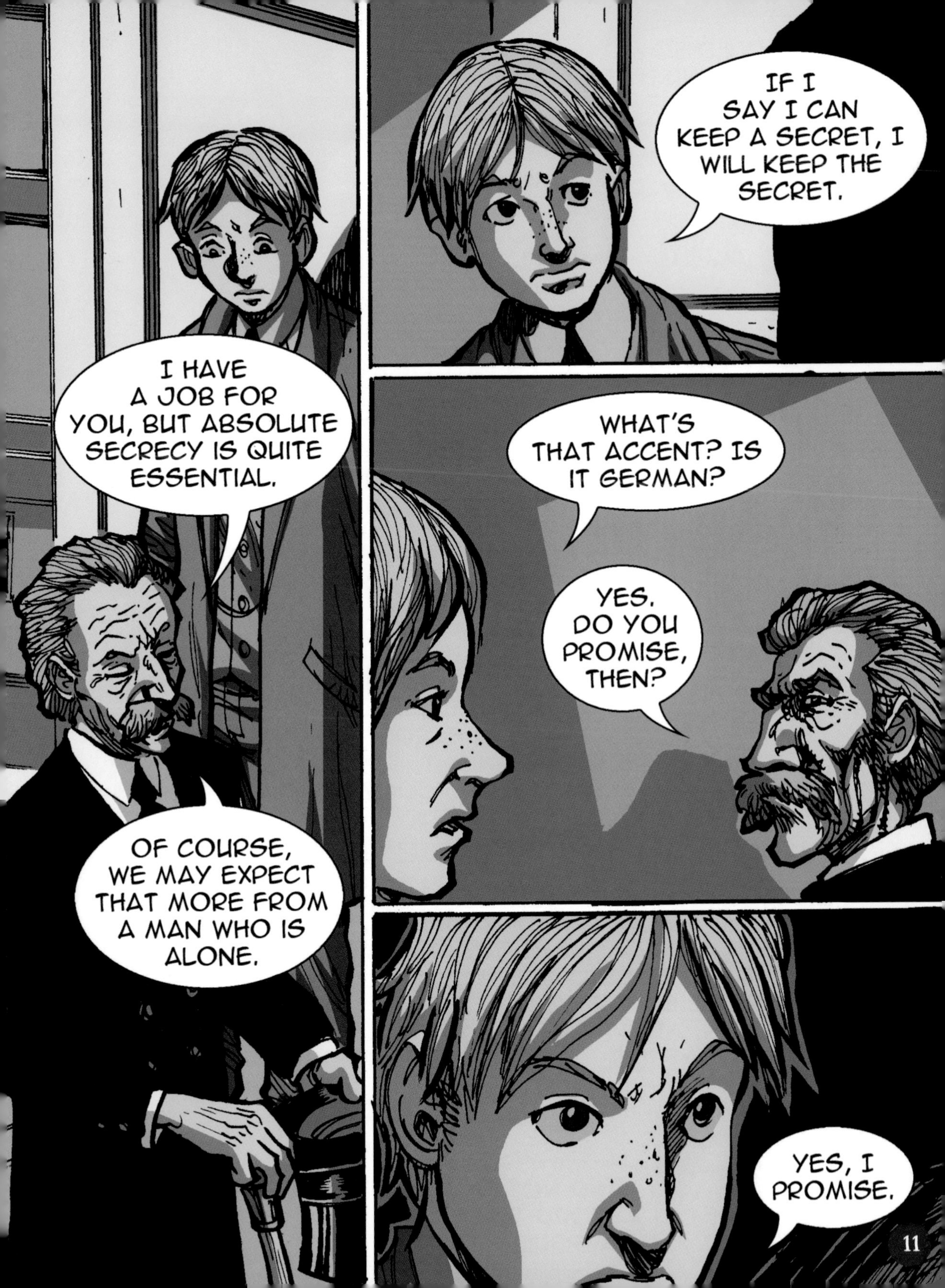
I HAVE A JOB FOR YOU, BUT ABSOLUTE SECRECY IS QUITE ESSENTIAL.
OF COURSE, WE MAY EXPECT THAT MORE FROM A MAN WHO IS ALONE.
IF I SAY I CAN KEEP A SECRET, I WILL KEEP THE SECRET.
WHAT'S THAT ACCENT? IS IT GERMAN?
YES. DO YOU PROMISE, THEN?
YES, I PROMISE.

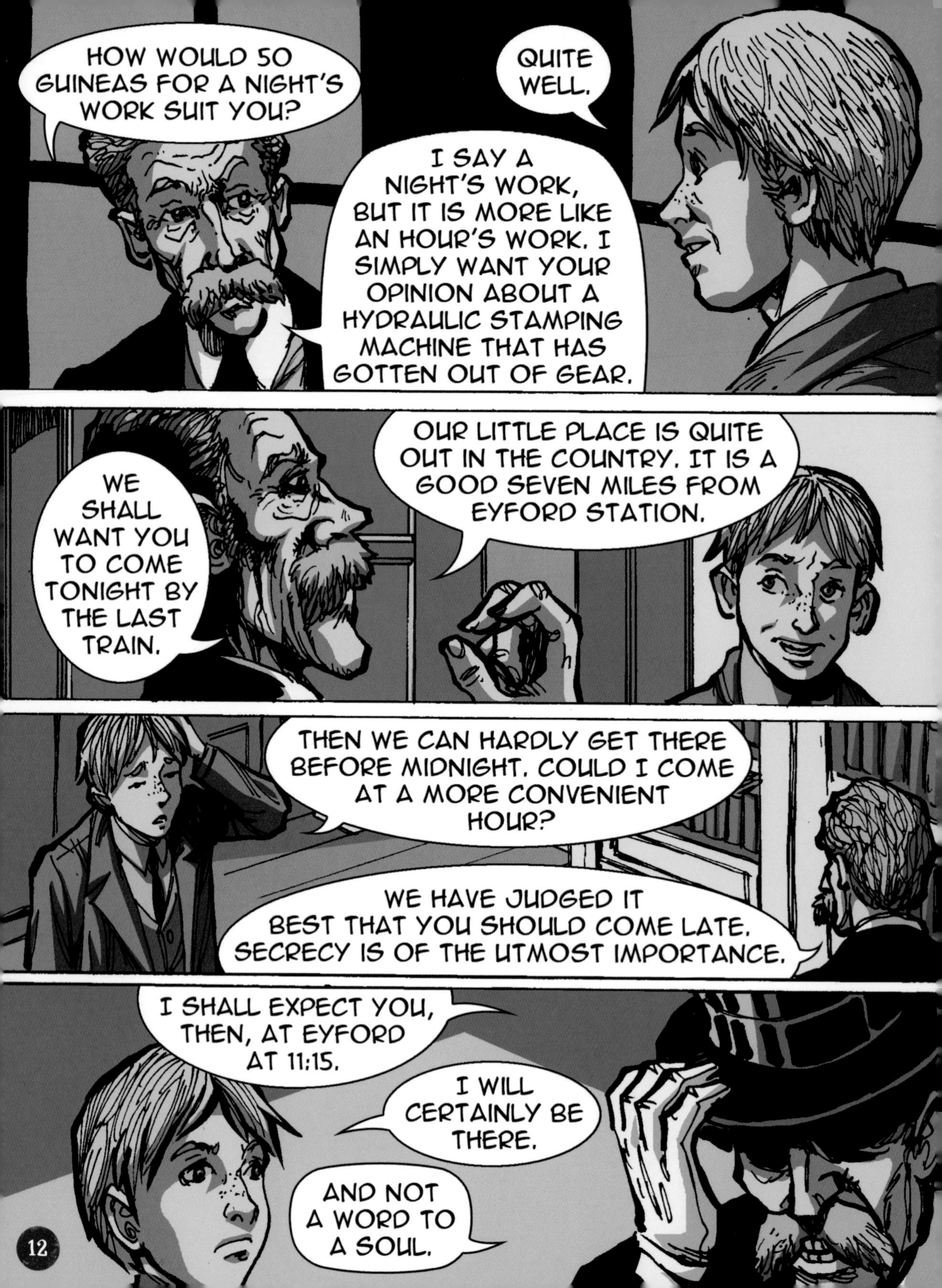
HOW WOULD 50 GUINEAS FOR A NIGHT'S WORK SUIT YOU?
QUITE WELL.
I SAY A NIGHT'S WORK, BUT IT IS MORE LIKE AN HOUR'S WORK. I SIMPLY WANT YOUR OPINION ABOUT A HYDRAULIC STAMPING MACHINE THAT HAS GOTTEN OUT OF GEAR.
WE SHALL WANT YOU TO COME TONIGHT BY THE LAST TRAIN.
OUR LITTLE PLACE IS QUITE OUT IN THE COUNTRY. IT IS A GOOD SEVEN MILES FROM EYFORD STATION.
THEN WE CAN HARDLY GET THERE BEFORE MIDNIGHT. COULD I COME AT A MORE CONVENIENT HOUR?
WE HAVE JUDGED IT BEST THAT YOU SHOULD COME LATE. SECRECY IS OF THE UTMOST IMPORTANCE.
I SHALL EXPECT YOU, THEN, AT EYFORD AT 11:15.
I WILL CERTAINLY BE THERE.
AND NOT A WORD TO A SOUL.

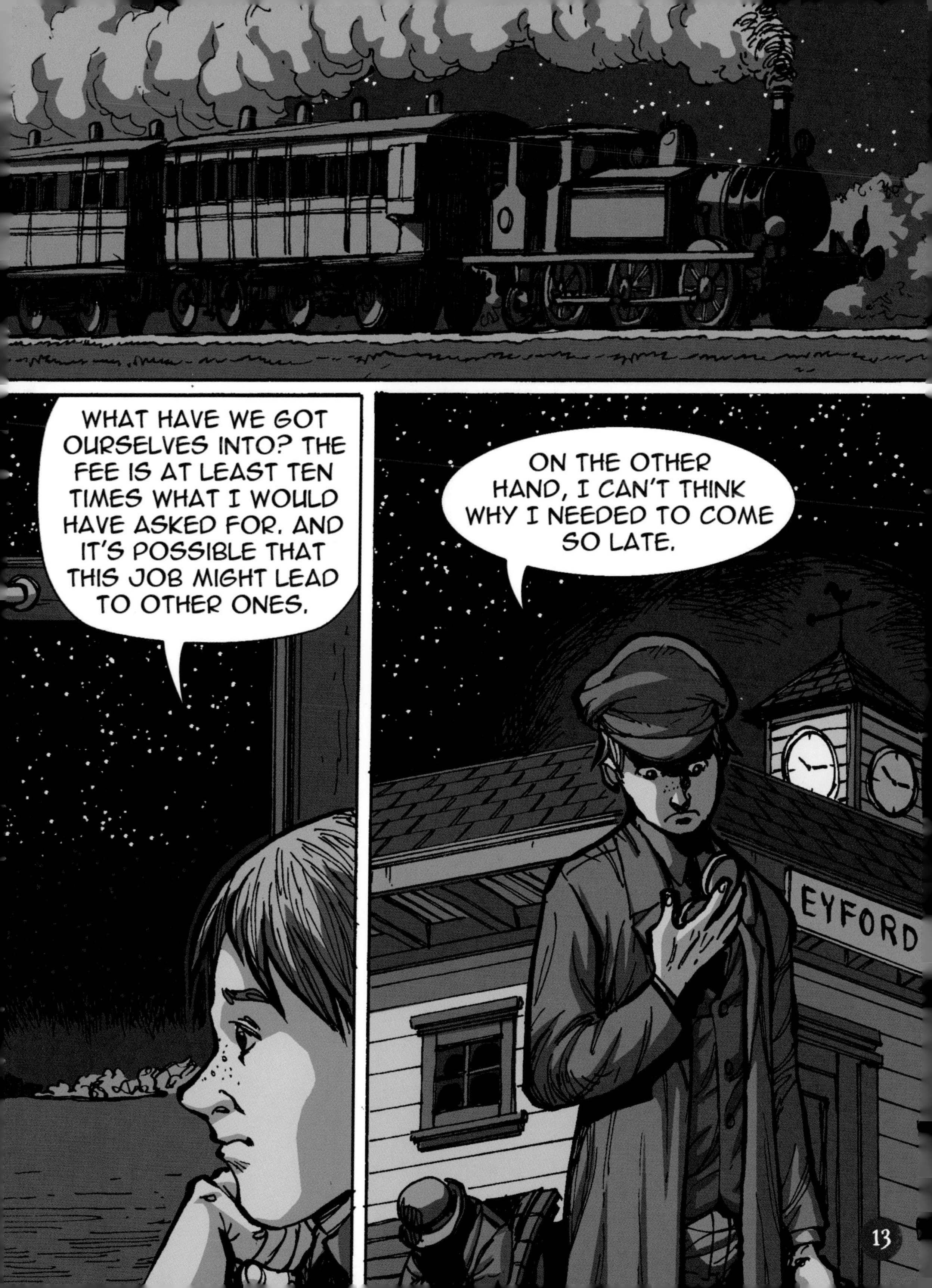
WHAT HAVE WE GOT OURSELVES INTO? THE FEE IS AT LEAST TEN TIMES WHAT I WOULD HAVE ASKED FOR. AND IT'S POSSIBLE THAT THIS JOB MIGHT LEAD TO OTHER ONES.
ON THE OTHER HAND, I CAN'T THINK WHY I NEEDED TO COME SO LATE.
EYFORD

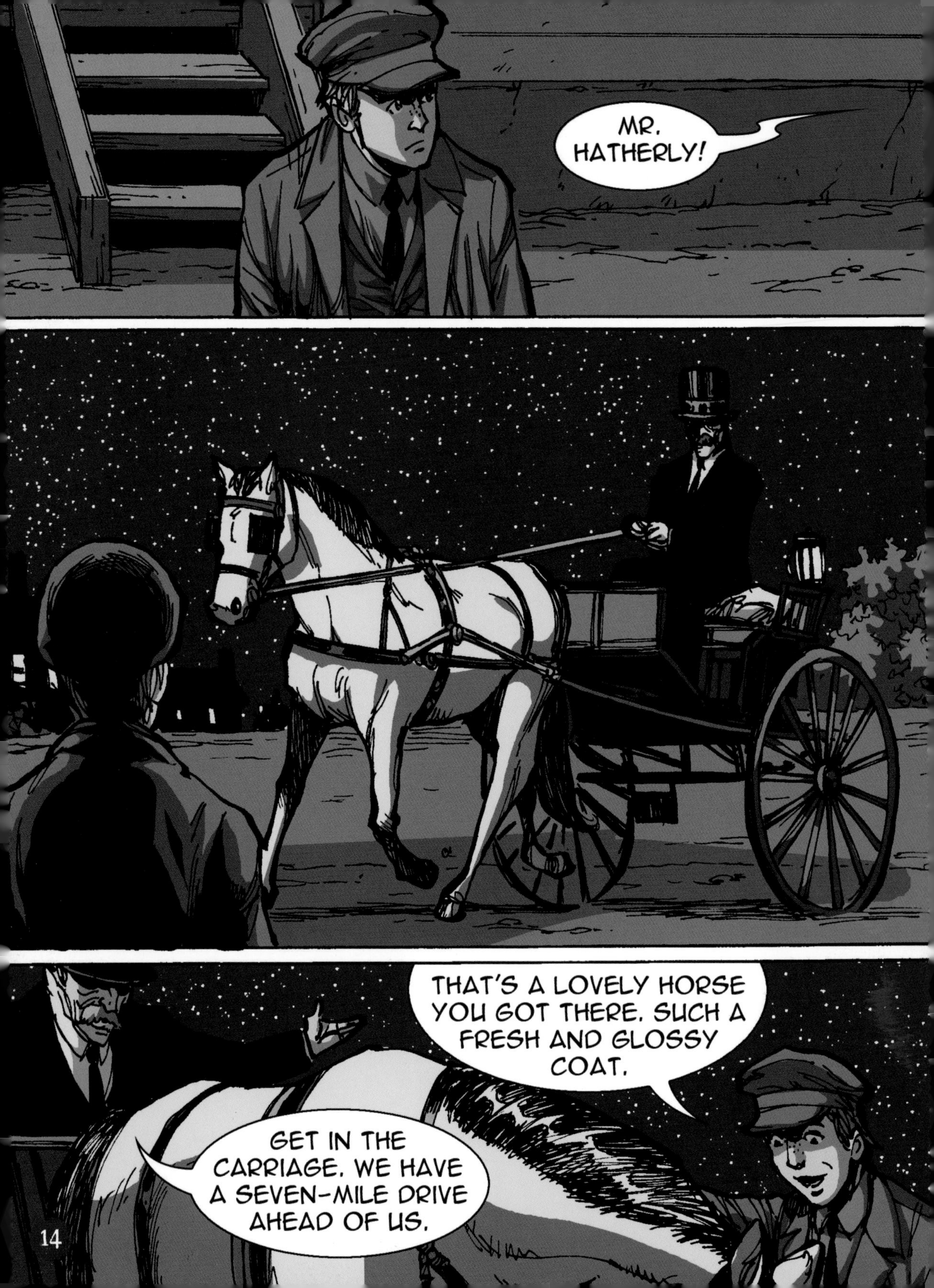
MR. HATHERLY!
THAT'S A LOVELY HORSE YOU GOT THERE. SUCH A FRESH AND GLOSSY COAT.
GET IN THE CARRIAGE. WE HAVE A SEVEN-MILE DRIVE AHEAD OF US.

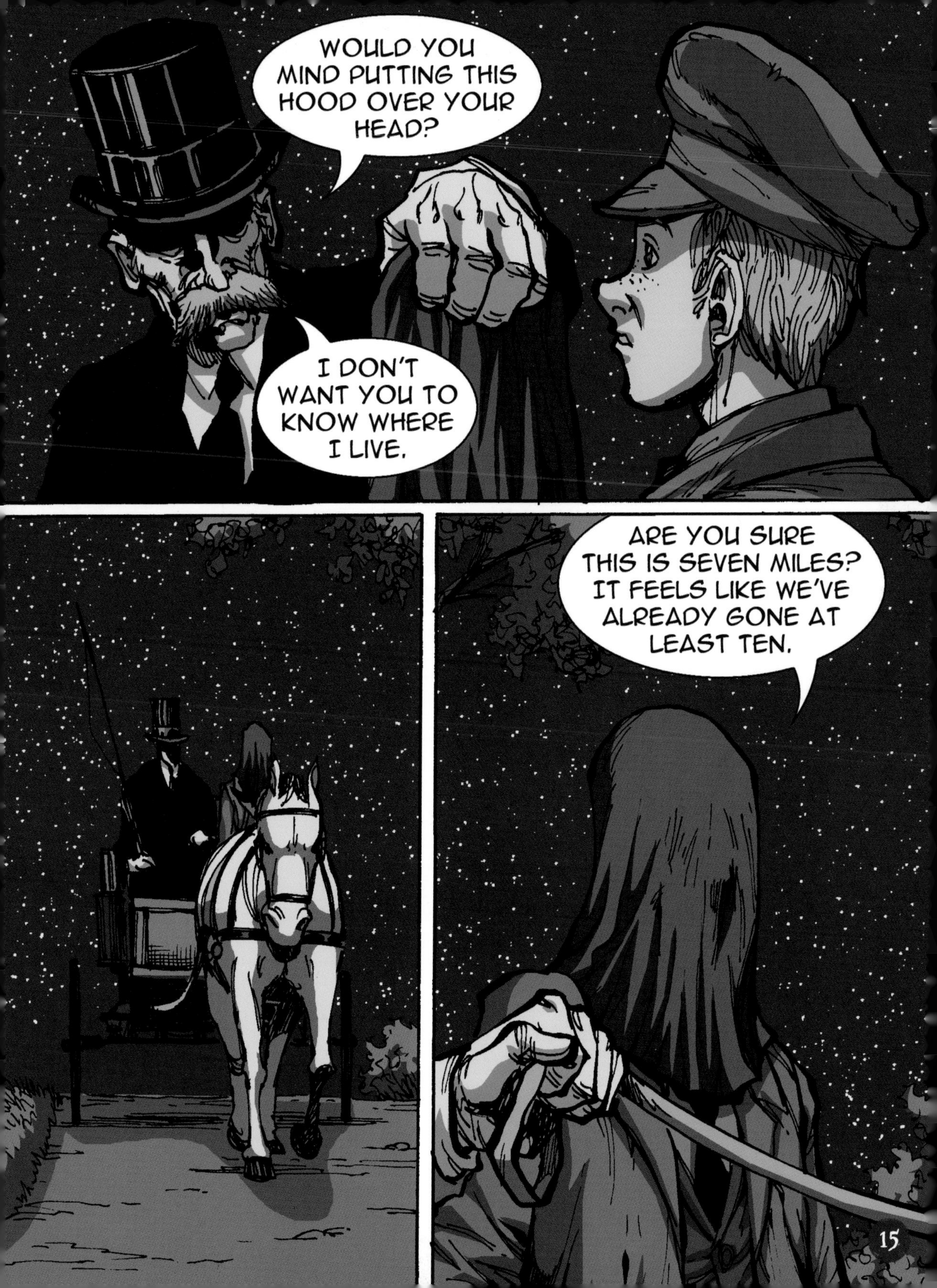
WOULD YOU MIND PUTTING THIS HOOD OVER YOUR HEAD?
I DON'T WANT YOU TO KNOW WHERE I LIVE.
ARE YOU SURE THIS IS SEVEN MILES? IT FEELS LIKE WE'VE ALREADY GONE AT LEAST TEN.

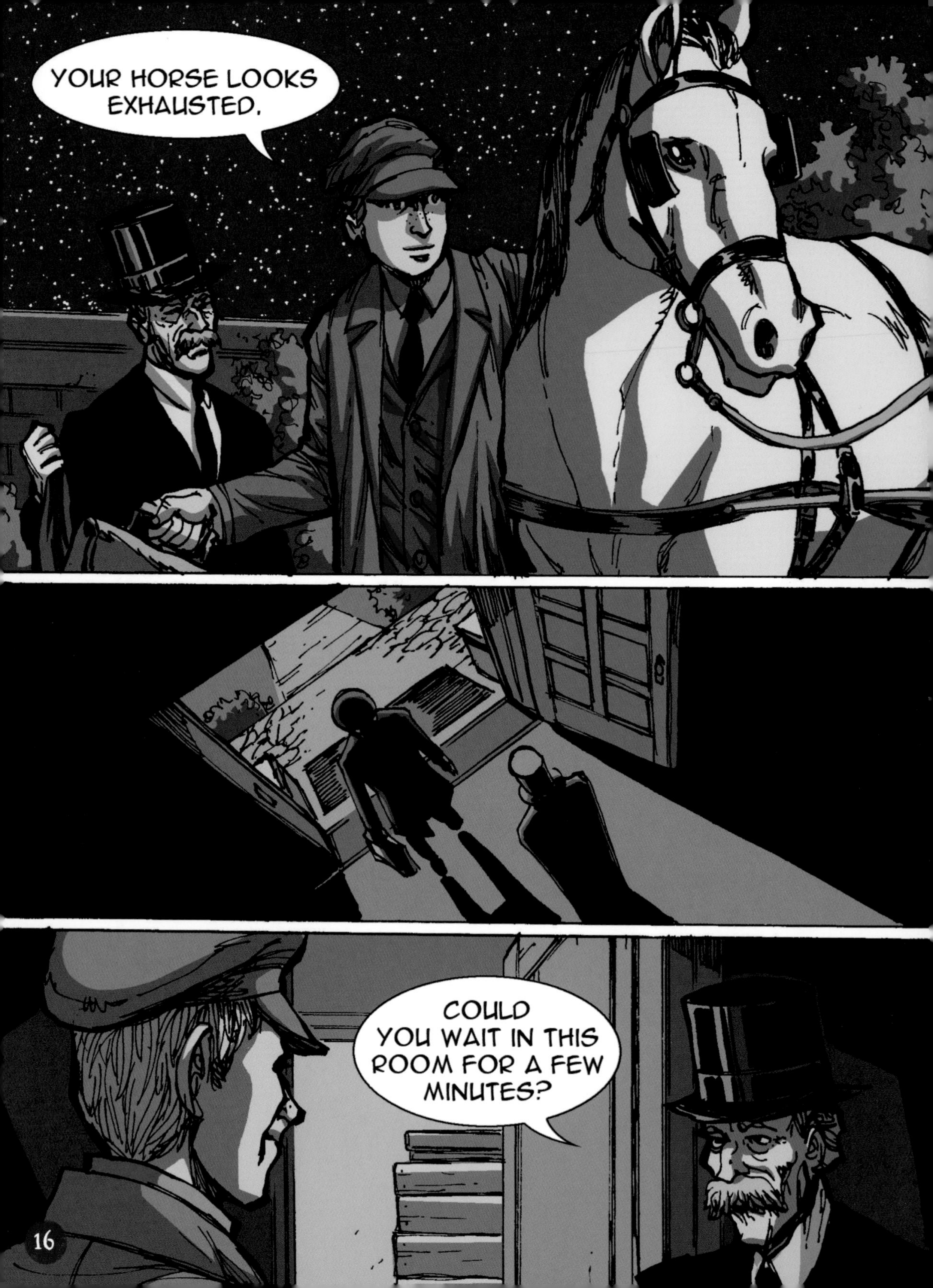
YOUR HORSE LOOKS EXHAUSTED.
COULD YOU WAIT IN THIS ROOM FOR A FEW MINUTES?

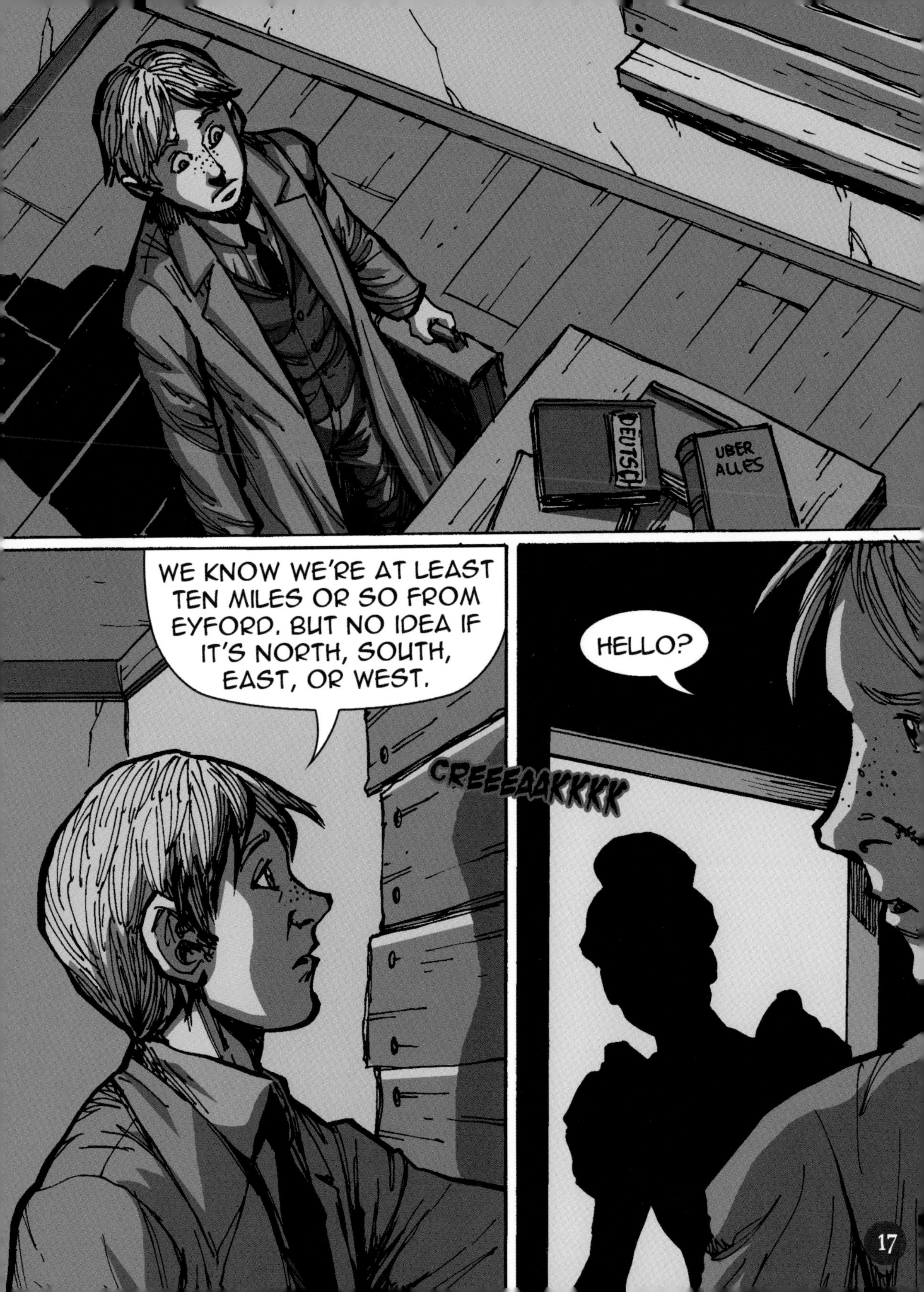
DEUTSCH
UBER ALLES
WE KNOW WE'RE AT LEAST TEN MILES OR SO FROM EYFORD. BUT NO IDEA IF IT'S NORTH, SOUTH, EAST, OR WEST.
CREEEAAKKKK
HELLO?

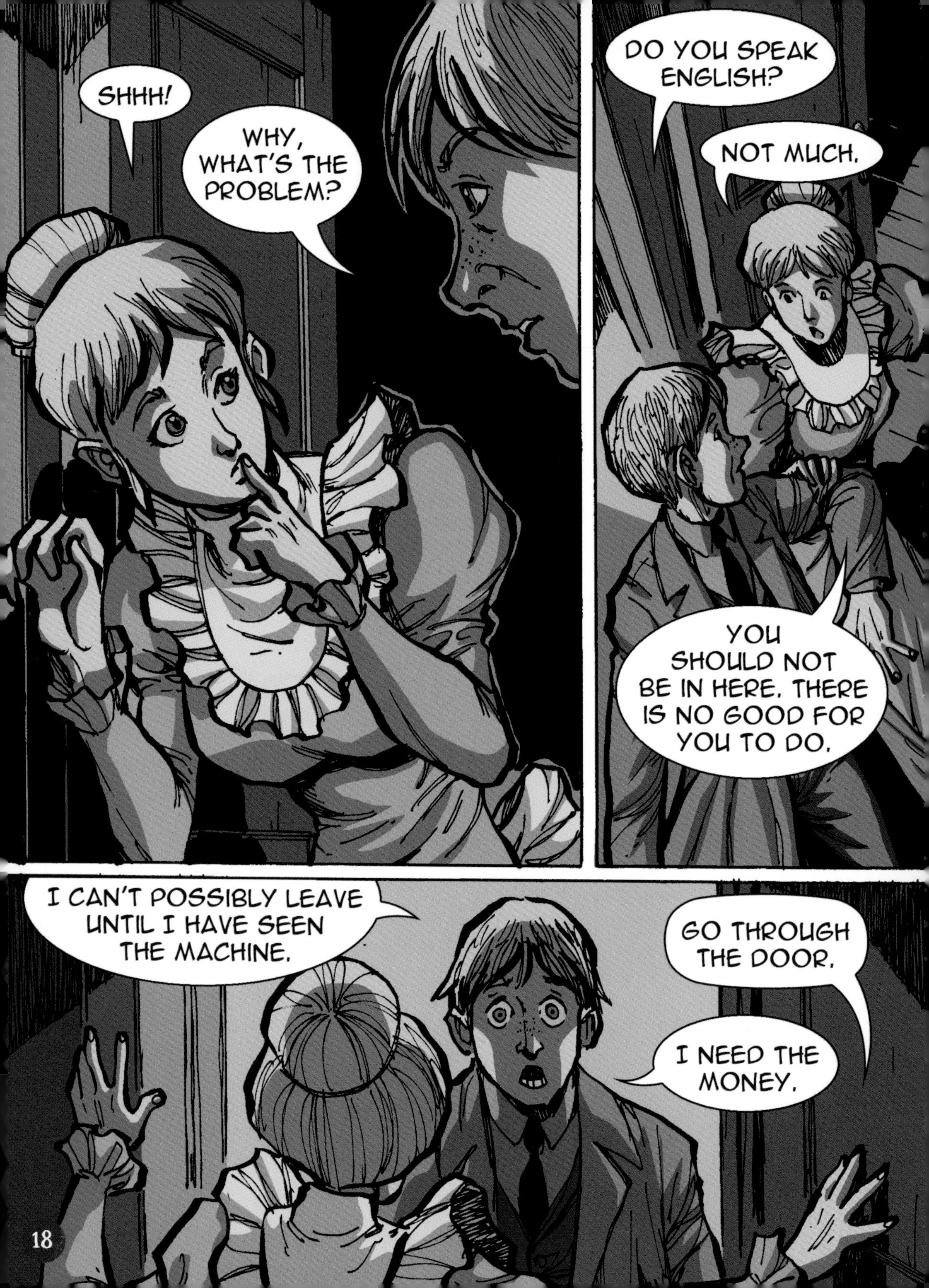
SHHH!
WHY, WHAT'S THE PROBLEM?
DO YOU SPEAK ENGLISH?
NOT MUCH.
YOU SHOULD NOT BE IN HERE. THERE IS NO GOOD FOR YOU TO DO.
I CAN'T POSSIBLY LEAVE UNTIL I HAVE SEEN THE MACHINE.
GO THROUGH THE DOOR.
I NEED THE MONEY.

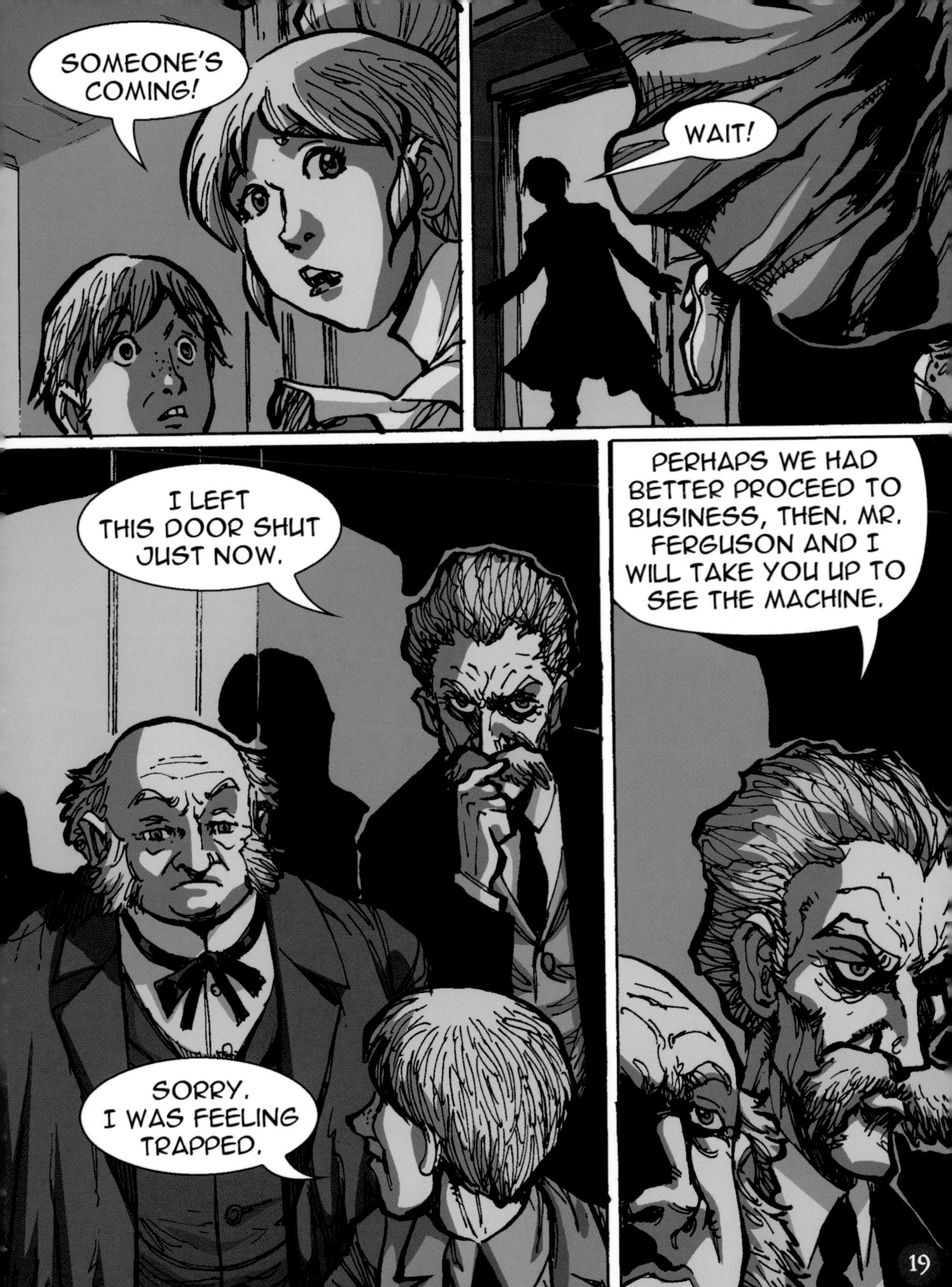
SOMEONE'S COMING!
WAIT!
I LEFT THIS DOOR SHUT JUST NOW.
SORRY. I WAS FEELING TRAPPED.
PERHAPS WE HAD BETTER PROCEED TO BUSINESS, THEN. MR. FERGUSON AND I WILL TAKE YOU UP TO SEE THE MACHINE.

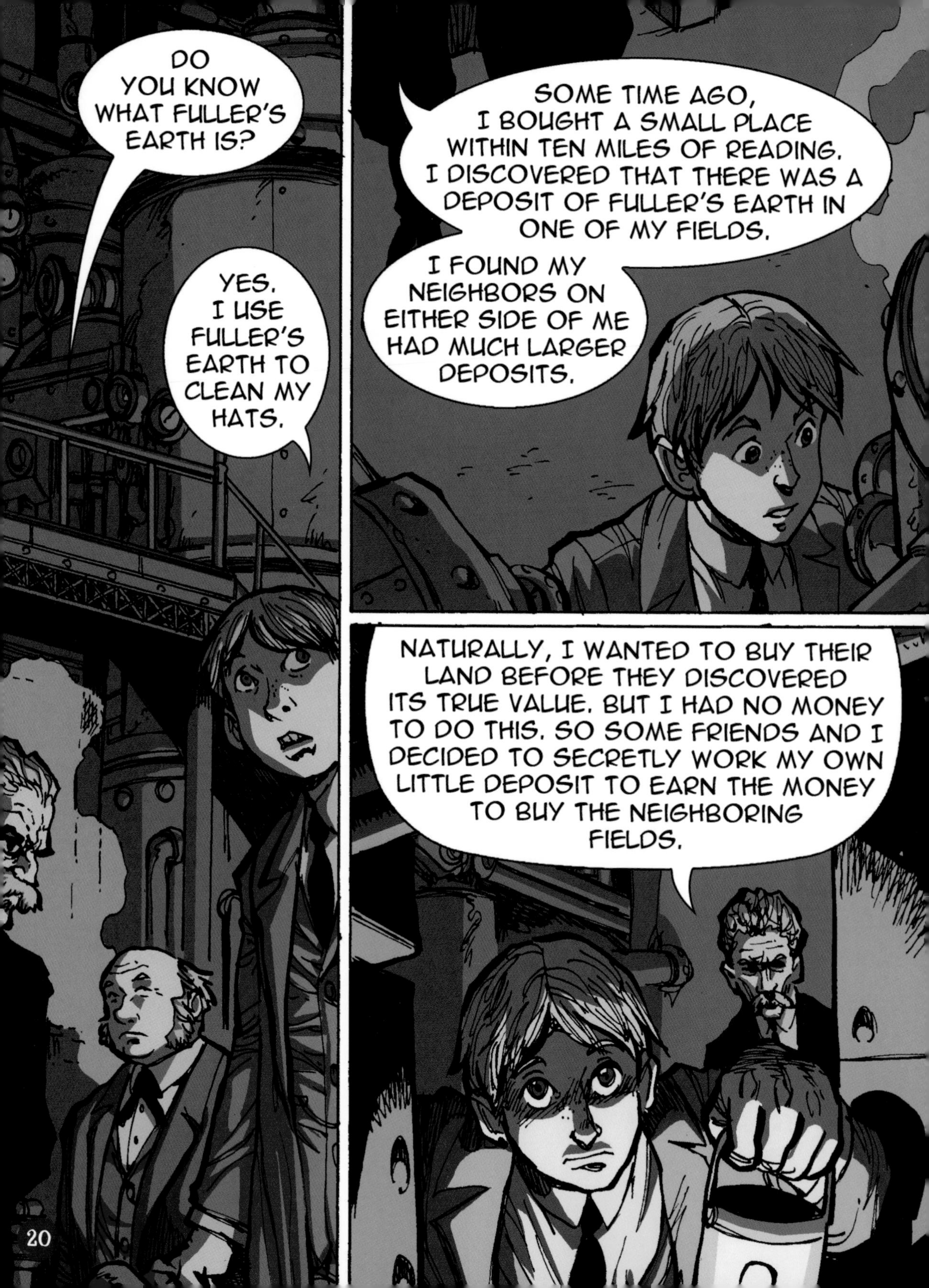
DO YOU KNOW WHAT FULLER'S EARTH IS?
YES. I USE FULLER'S EARTH TO CLEAN MY HATS.
SOME TIME AGO, I BOUGHT A SMALL PLACE WITHIN TEN MILES OF READING. I DISCOVERED THAT THERE WAS A DEPOSIT OF FULLER'S EARTH IN ONE OF MY FIELDS.
I FOUND MY NEIGHBORS ON EITHER SIDE OF ME HAD MUCH LARGER DEPOSITS.
NATURALLY, I WANTED TO BUY THEIR LAND BEFORE THEY DISCOVERED ITS TRUE VALUE. BUT I HAD NO MONEY TO DO THIS. SO SOME FRIENDS AND I DECIDED TO SECRETLY WORK MY OWN LITTLE DEPOSIT TO EARN THE MONEY TO BUY THE NEIGHBORING FIELDS.

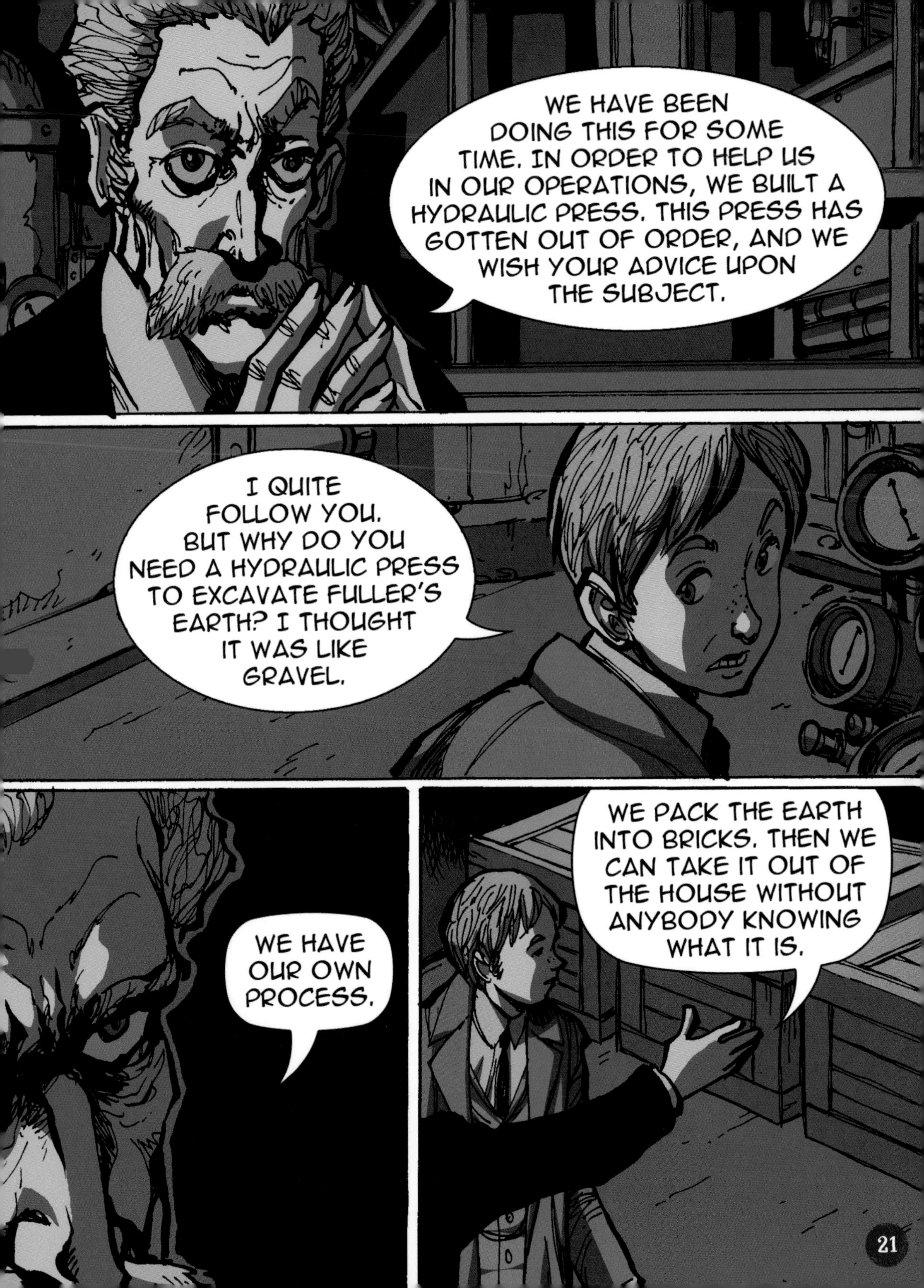
WE HAVE BEEN DOING THIS FOR SOME TIME. IN ORDER TO HELP US IN OUR OPERATIONS, WE BUILT A HYDRAULIC PRESS. THIS PRESS HAS GOTTEN OUT OF ORDER, AND WE WISH YOUR ADVICE UPON THE SUBJECT.
I QUITE FOLLOW YOU. BUT WHY DO YOU NEED A HYDRAULIC PRESS TO EXCAVATE FULLER'S EARTH? I THOUGHT IT WAS LIKE GRAVEL.
WE HAVE OUR OWN PROCESS.
WE PACK THE EARTH INTO BRICKS. THEN WE CAN TAKE IT OUT OF THE HOUSE WITHOUT ANYBODY KNOWING WHAT IT IS.

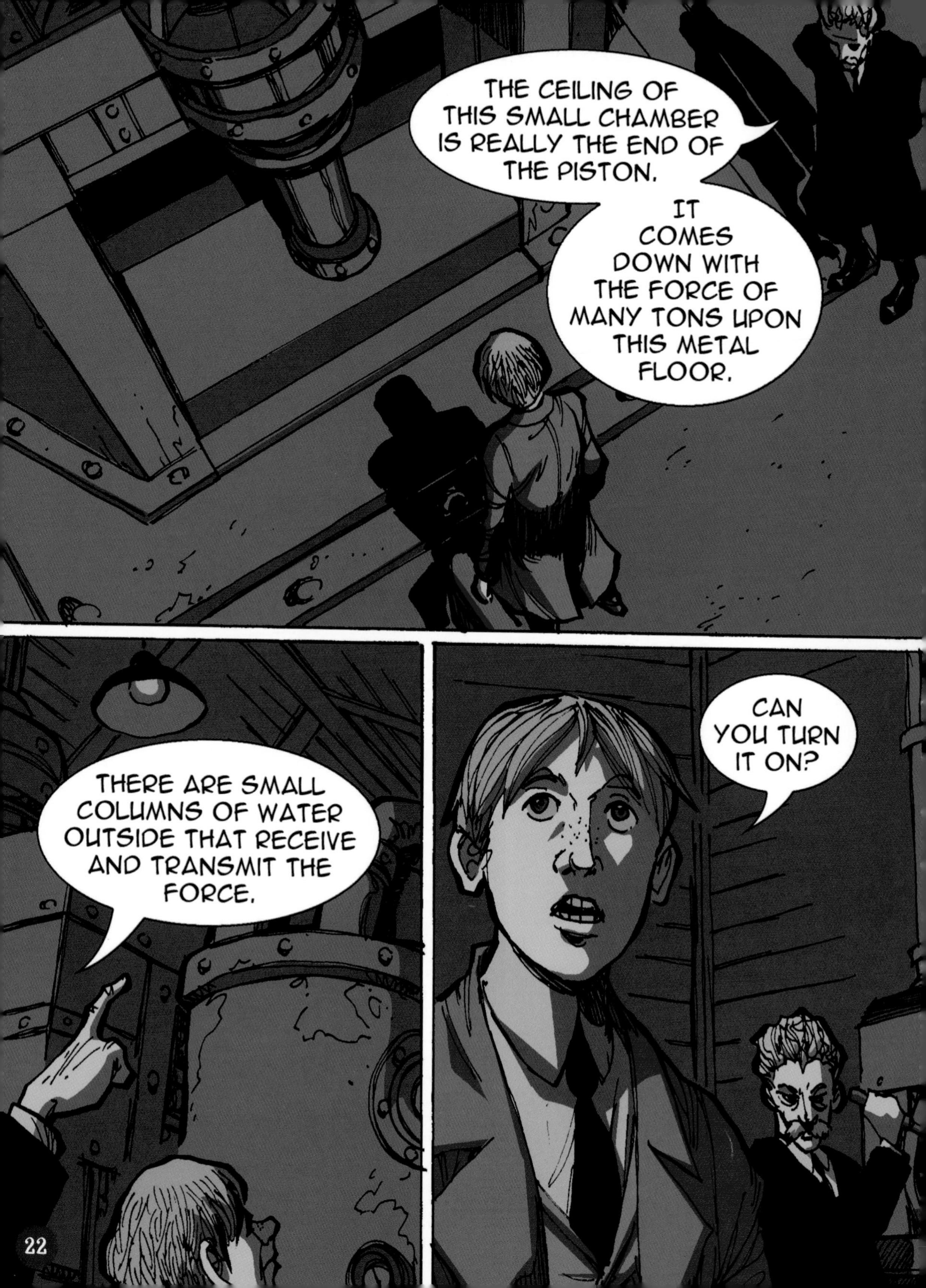
THE CEILING OF THIS SMALL CHAMBER IS REALLY THE END OF THE PISTON.
IT COMES DOWN WITH THE FORCE OF MANY TONS UPON THIS METAL FLOOR.
THERE ARE SMALL COLUMNS OF WATER OUTSIDE THAT RECEIVE AND TRANSMIT THE FORCE.
CAN YOU TURN IT ON?

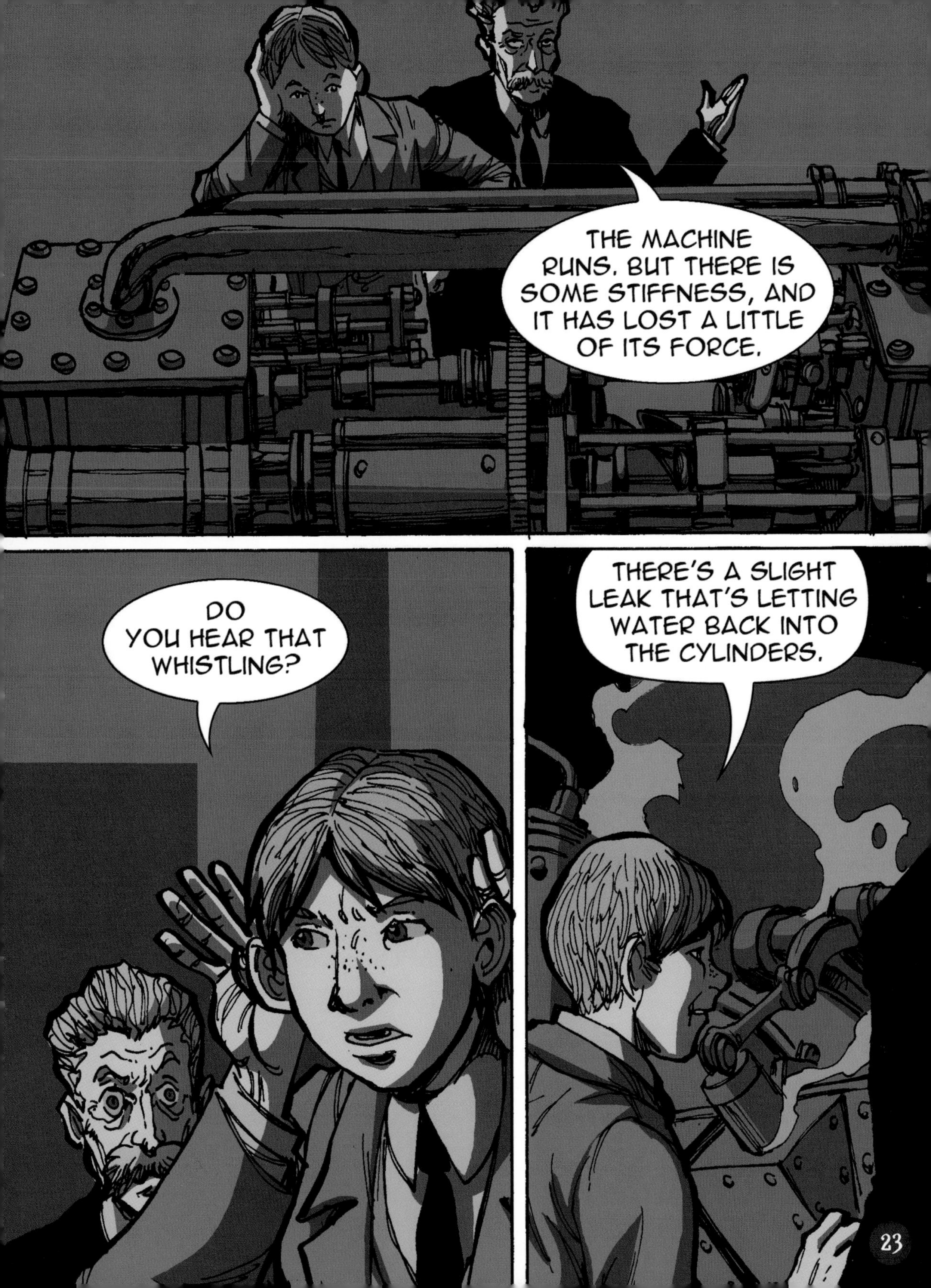
THE MACHINE RUNS. BUT THERE IS SOME STIFFNESS, AND IT HAS LOST A LITTLE OF ITS FORCE.
DO YOU HEAR THAT WHISTLING?
THERE'S A SLIGHT LEAK THAT'S LETTING WATER BACK INTO THE CYLINDERS.

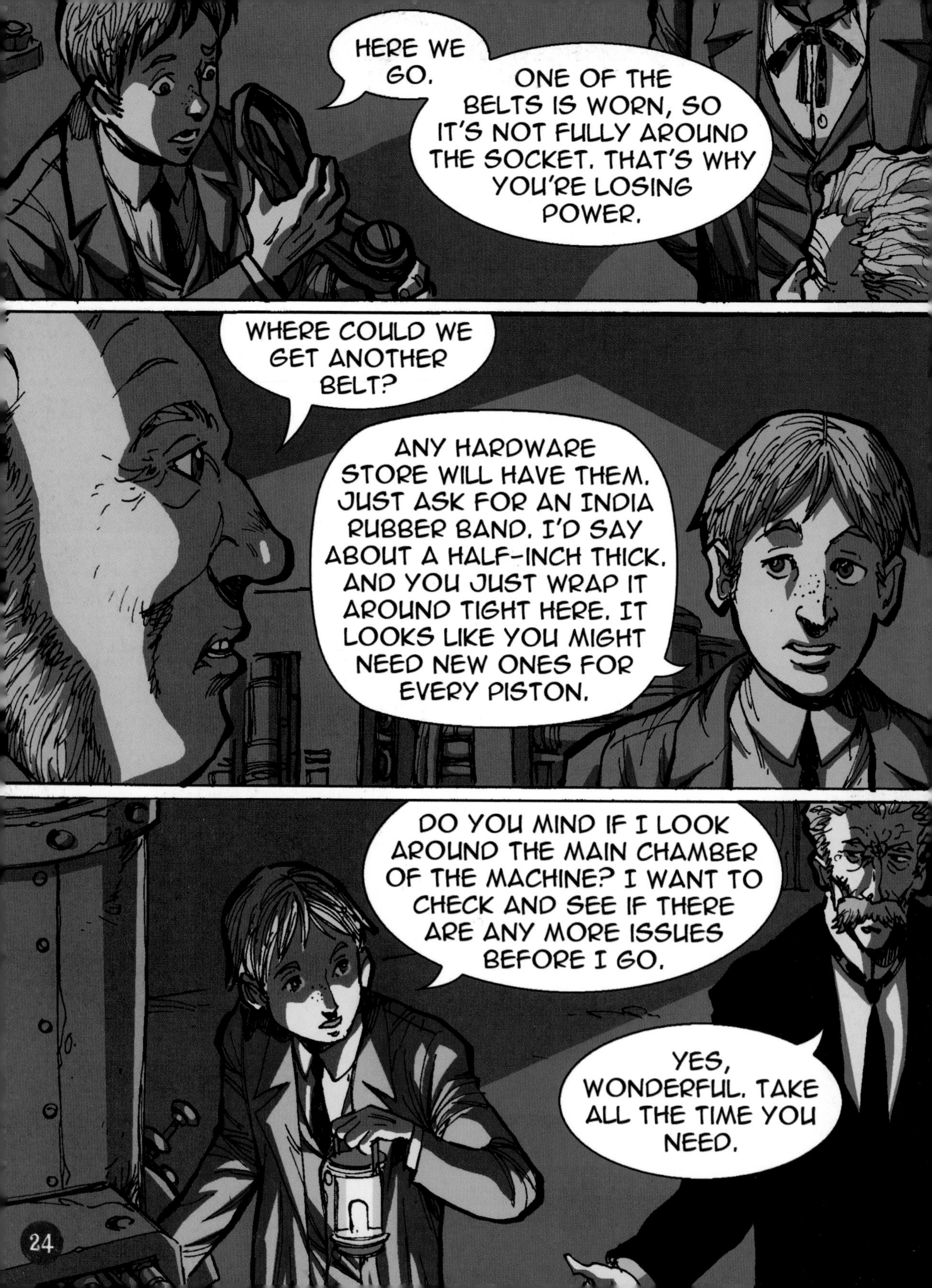
HERE WE GO.
ONE OF THE BELTS IS WORN, SO IT'S NOT FULLY AROUND THE SOCKET. THAT'S WHY YOU'RE LOSING POWER.
WHERE COULD WE GET ANOTHER BELT?
ANY HARDWARE STORE WILL HAVE THEM. JUST ASK FOR AN INDIA RUBBER BAND. I'D SAY ABOUT A HALF-INCH THICK. AND YOU JUST WRAP IT AROUND TIGHT HERE. IT LOOKS LIKE YOU MIGHT NEED NEW ONES FOR EVERY PISTON.
DO YOU MIND IF I LOOK AROUND THE MAIN CHAMBER OF THE MACHINE? I WANT TO CHECK AND SEE IF THERE ARE ANY MORE ISSUES BEFORE I GO.
YES, WONDERFUL. TAKE ALL THE TIME YOU NEED.

WELL, IT'S PRETTY CLEAR THE STORY OF THE FULLER'S EARTH IS A LIE. THIS MACHINE IS WAY TOO BIG.

WHAT IS THIS? MONEY?

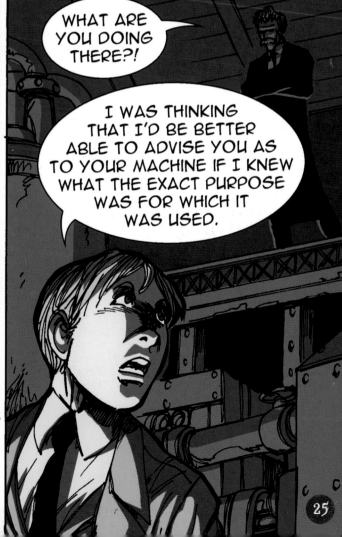

WHAT ARE YOU DOING THERE?!

I WAS THINKING THAT I'D BE BETTER ABLE TO ADVISE YOU AS TO YOUR MACHINE IF I KNEW WHAT THE EXACT PURPOSE WAS FOR WHICH IT WAS USED.

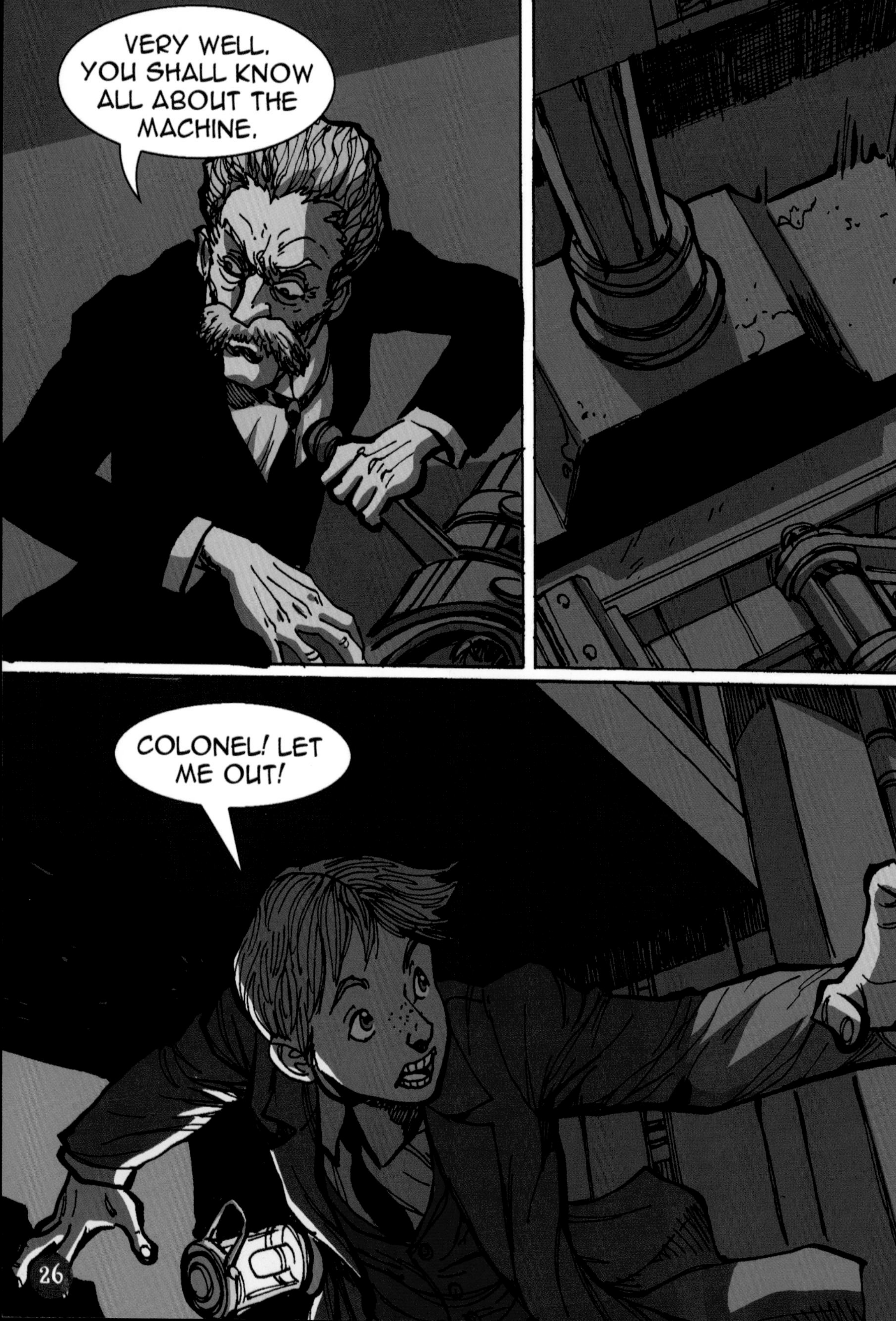
VERY WELL. YOU SHALL KNOW ALL ABOUT THE MACHINE.
COLONEL! LET ME OUT!

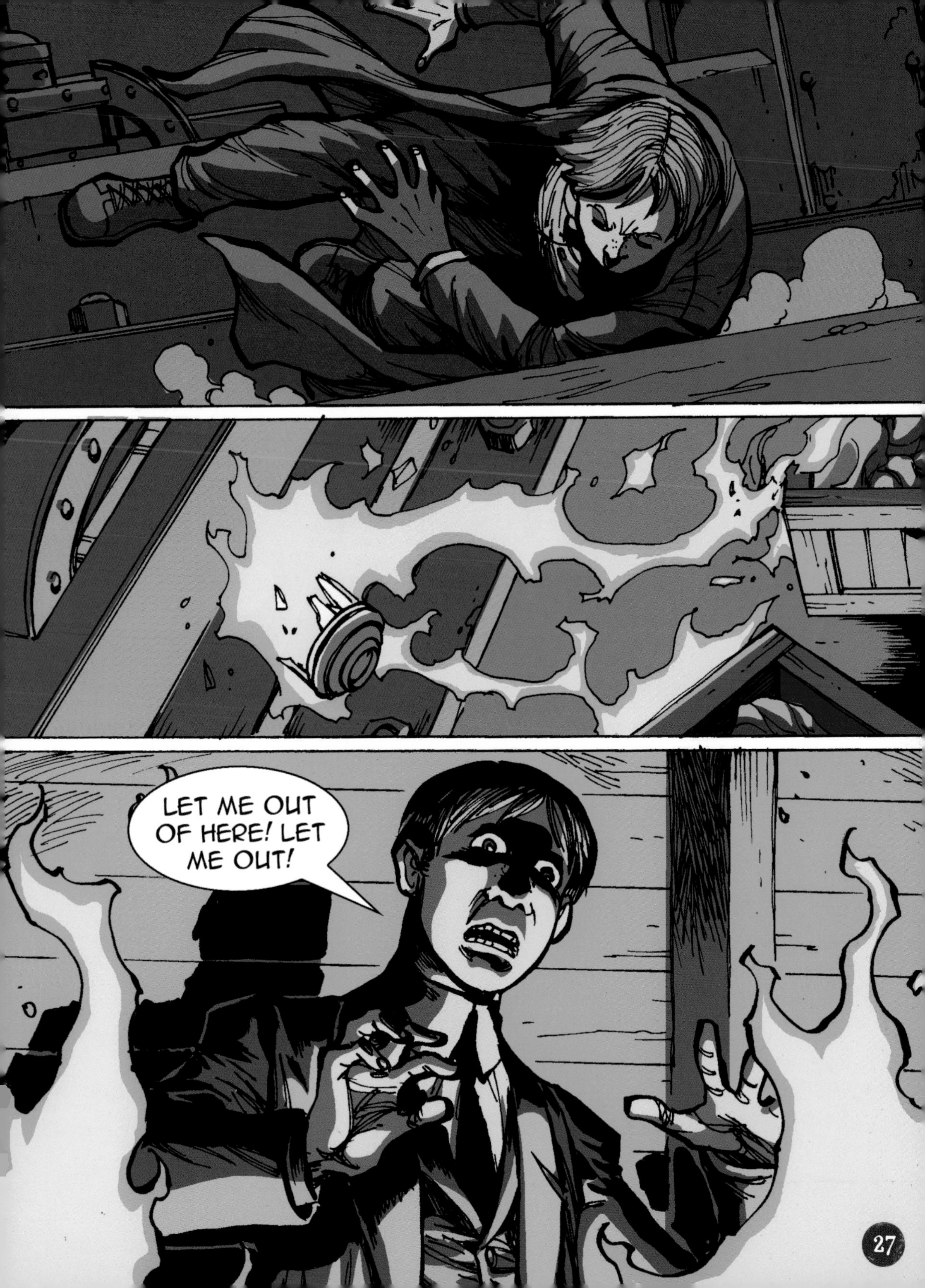
LET ME OUT OF HERE! LET ME OUT!

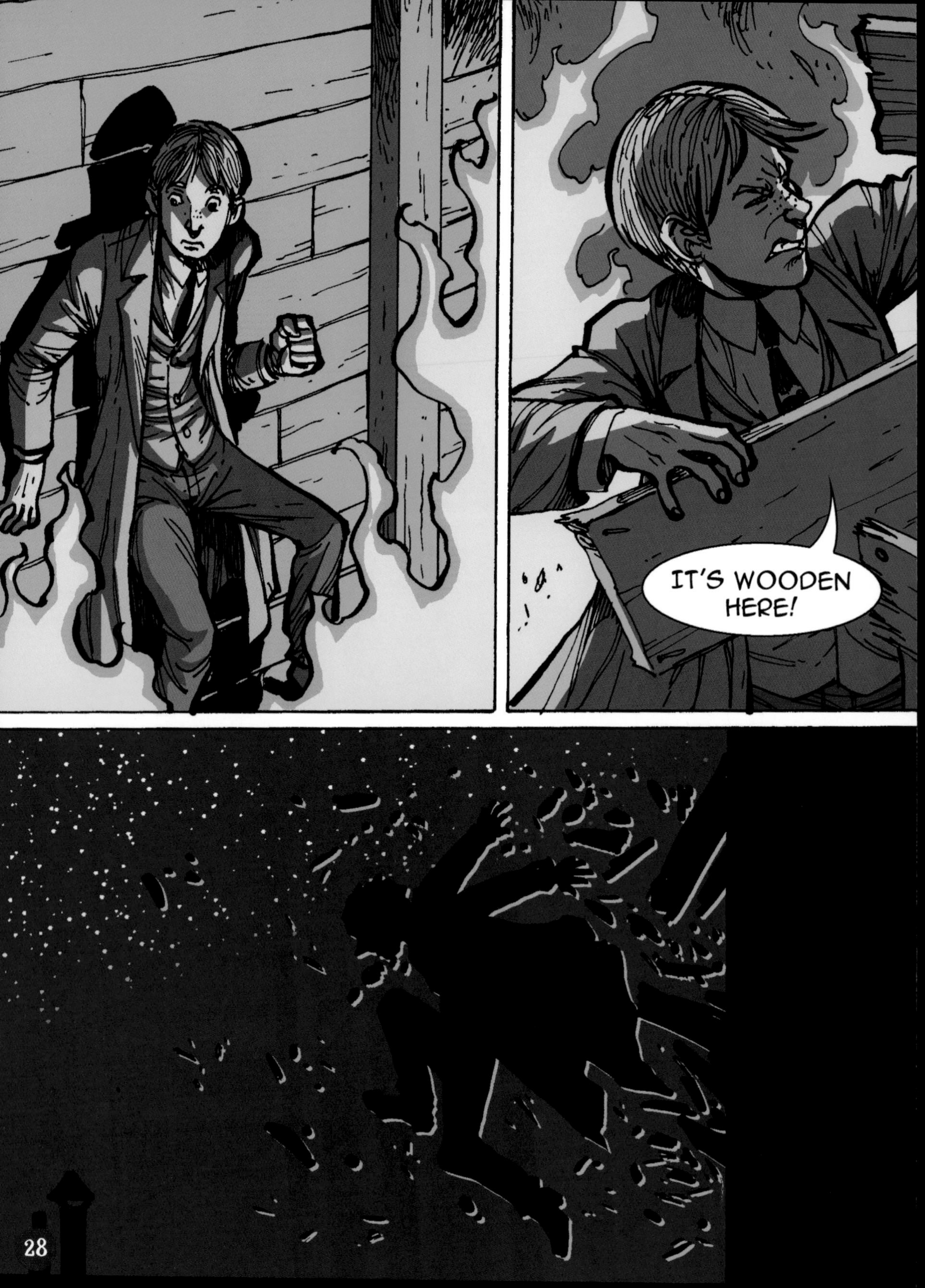
IT'S WOODEN HERE!

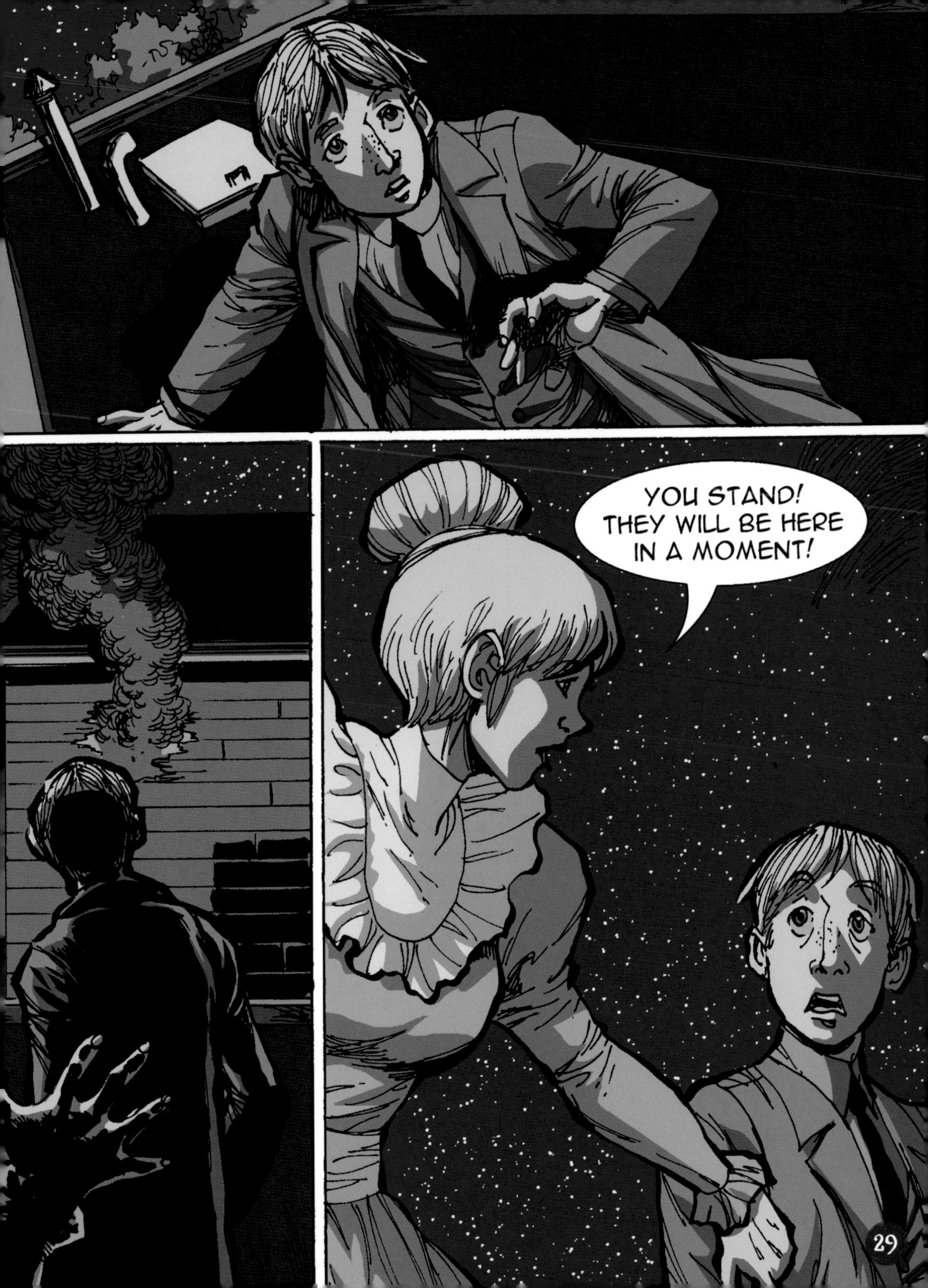
YOU STAND!
THEY WILL BE HERE
IN A MOMENT!

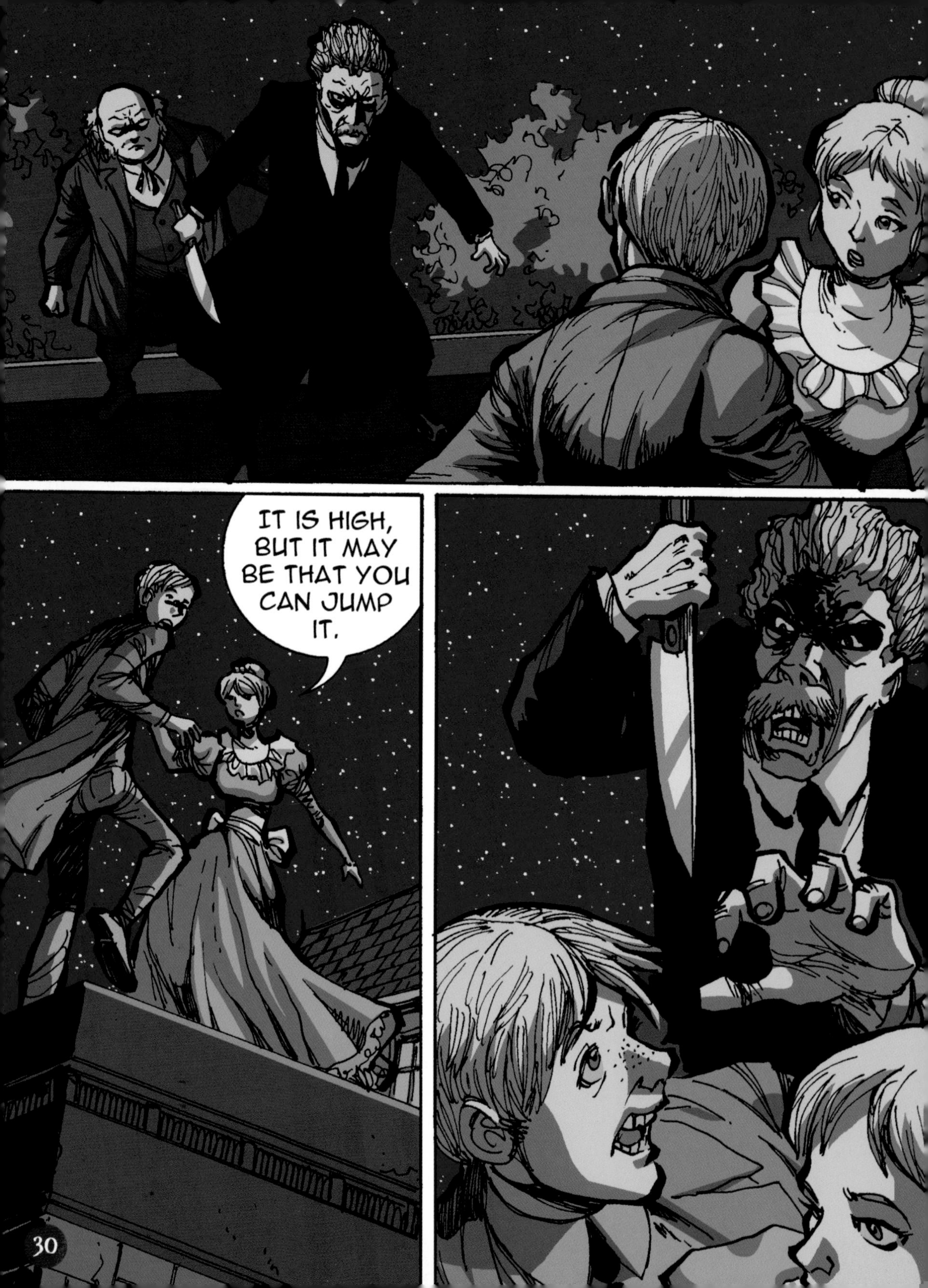
IT IS HIGH, BUT IT MAY BE THAT YOU CAN JUMP IT.

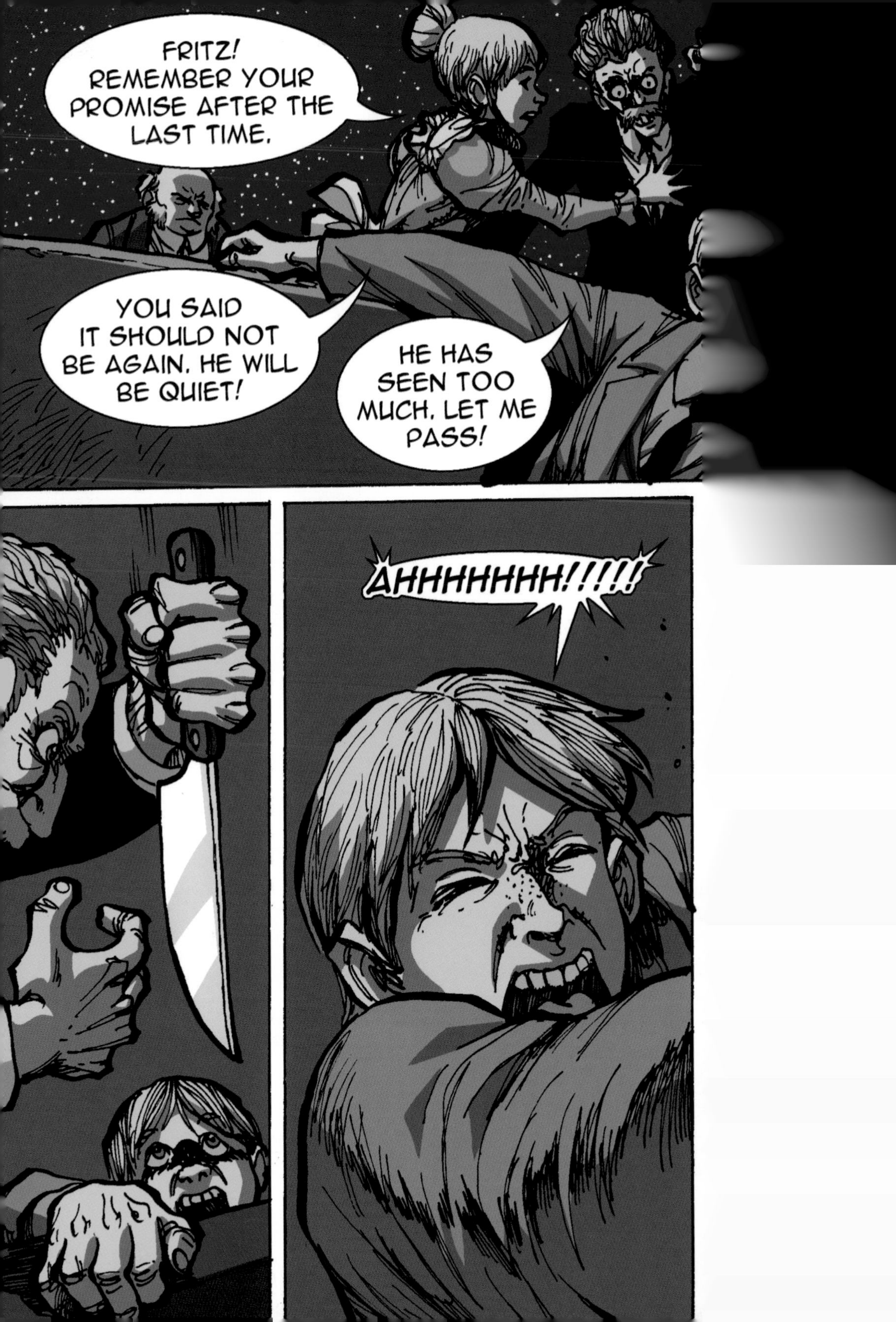
FRITZ! REMEMBER YOUR PROMISE AFTER THE LAST TIME.
YOU SAID IT SHOULD NOT BE AGAIN. HE WILL BE QUIET!
HE HAS SEEN TOO MUCH. LET ME PASS!
AHHHHHHH!!!!!

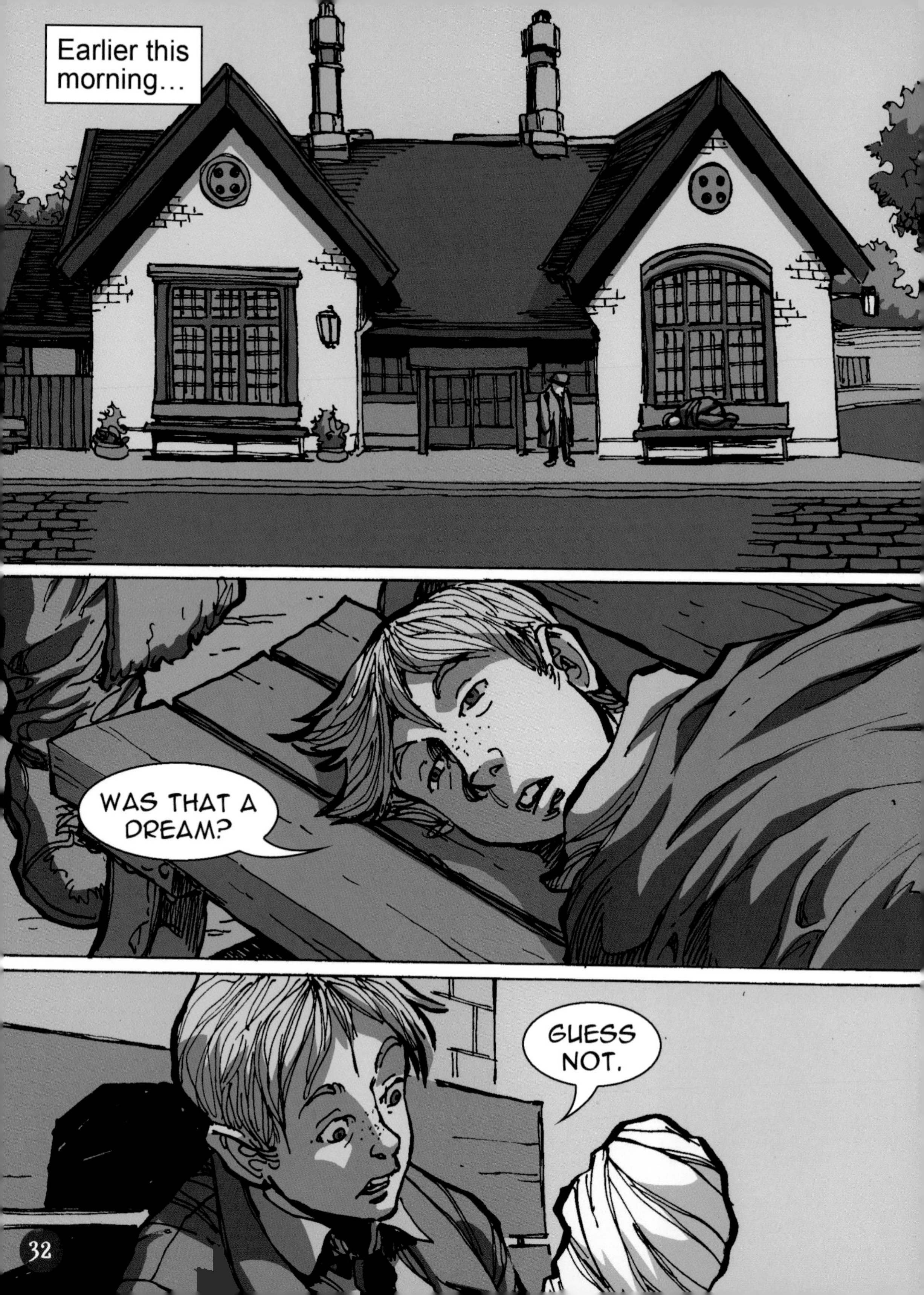
Earlier this morning...
WAS THAT A DREAM?
GUESS NOT.

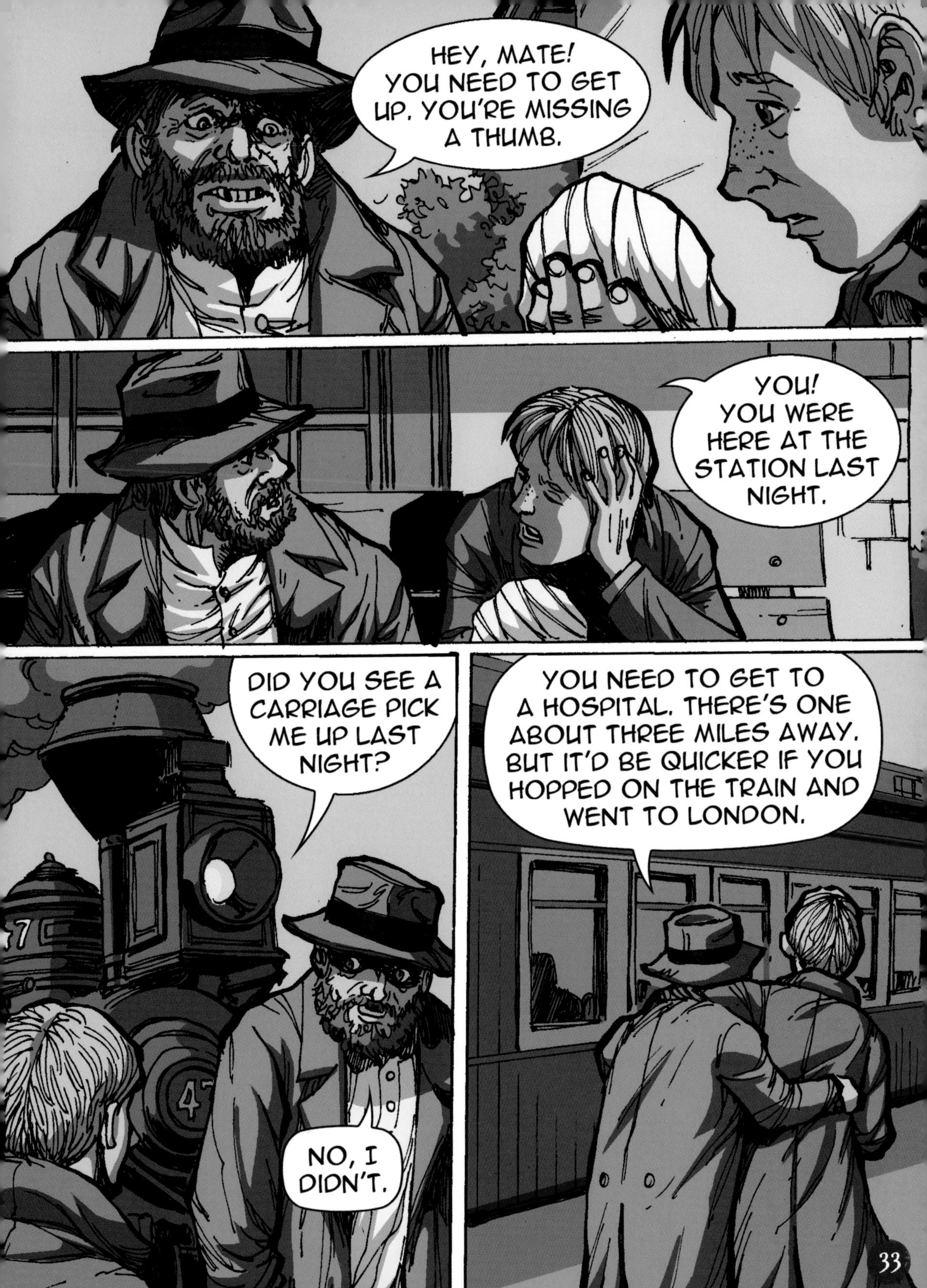
HEY, MATE! YOU NEED TO GET UP. YOU'RE MISSING A THUMB.
YOU! YOU WERE HERE AT THE STATION LAST NIGHT.
DID YOU SEE A CARRIAGE PICK ME UP LAST NIGHT?
NO, I DIDN'T.
YOU NEED TO GET TO A HOSPITAL. THERE'S ONE ABOUT THREE MILES AWAY. BUT IT'D BE QUICKER IF YOU HOPPED ON THE TRAIN AND WENT TO LONDON.
47

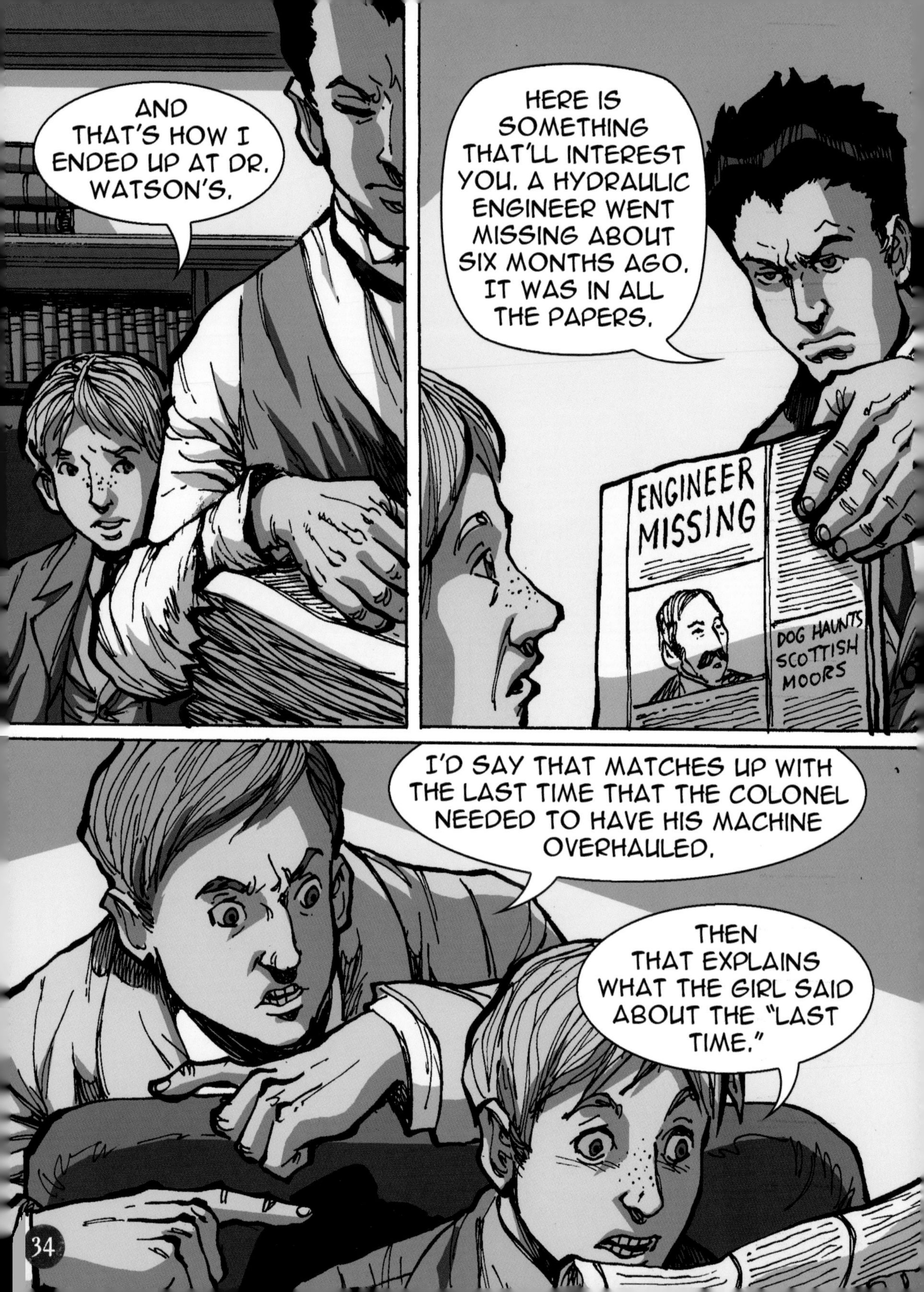
AND THAT'S HOW I ENDED UP AT DR. WATSON'S.
HERE IS SOMETHING THAT'LL INTEREST YOU. A HYDRAULIC ENGINEER WENT MISSING ABOUT SIX MONTHS AGO. IT WAS IN ALL THE PAPERS.
ENGINEER MISSING
DOG HAUNTS SCOTTISH MOORS
I'D SAY THAT MATCHES UP WITH THE LAST TIME THAT THE COLONEL NEEDED TO HAVE HIS MACHINE OVERHAULED.
THEN THAT EXPLAINS WHAT THE GIRL SAID ABOUT THE "LAST TIME."

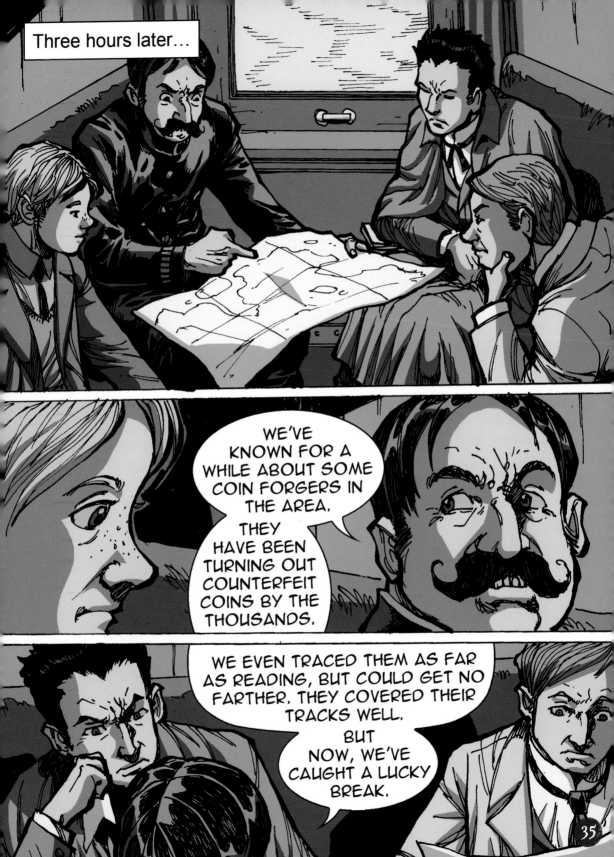

Three hours later...

WE'VE KNOWN FOR A WHILE ABOUT SOME COIN FORGERS IN THE AREA.

THEY HAVE BEEN TURNING OUT COUNTERFEIT COINS BY THE THOUSANDS.

WE EVEN TRACED THEM AS FAR AS READING, BUT COULD GET NO FARTHER. THEY COVERED THEIR TRACKS WELL.

BUT NOW, WE'VE CAUGHT A LUCKY BREAK.

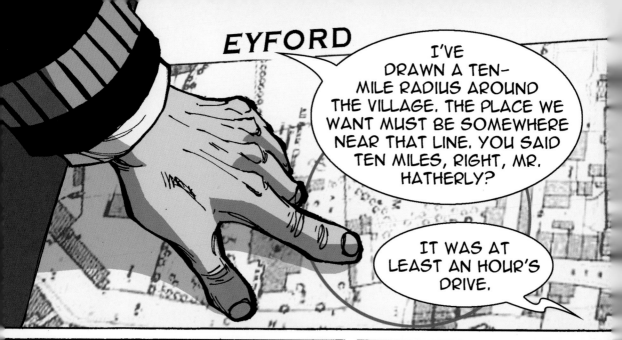

EYFORD

I'VE DRAWN A TEN-MILE RADIUS AROUND THE VILLAGE. THE PLACE WE WANT MUST BE SOMEWHERE NEAR THAT LINE. YOU SAID TEN MILES, RIGHT, MR. HATHERLY?

IT WAS AT LEAST AN HOUR'S DRIVE.

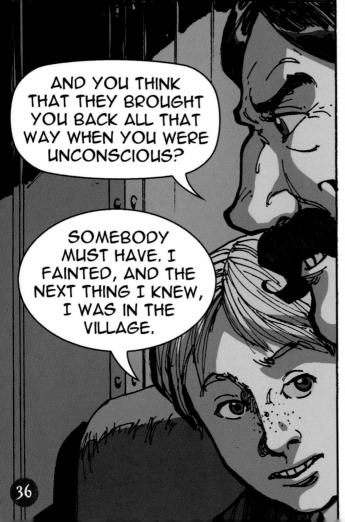

AND YOU THINK THAT THEY BROUGHT YOU BACK ALL THAT WAY WHEN YOU WERE UNCONSCIOUS?

SOMEBODY MUST HAVE. I FAINTED, AND THE NEXT THING I KNEW, I WAS IN THE VILLAGE.

WHAT I CANNOT UNDERSTAND IS WHY THEY WOULD LET YOU GO.

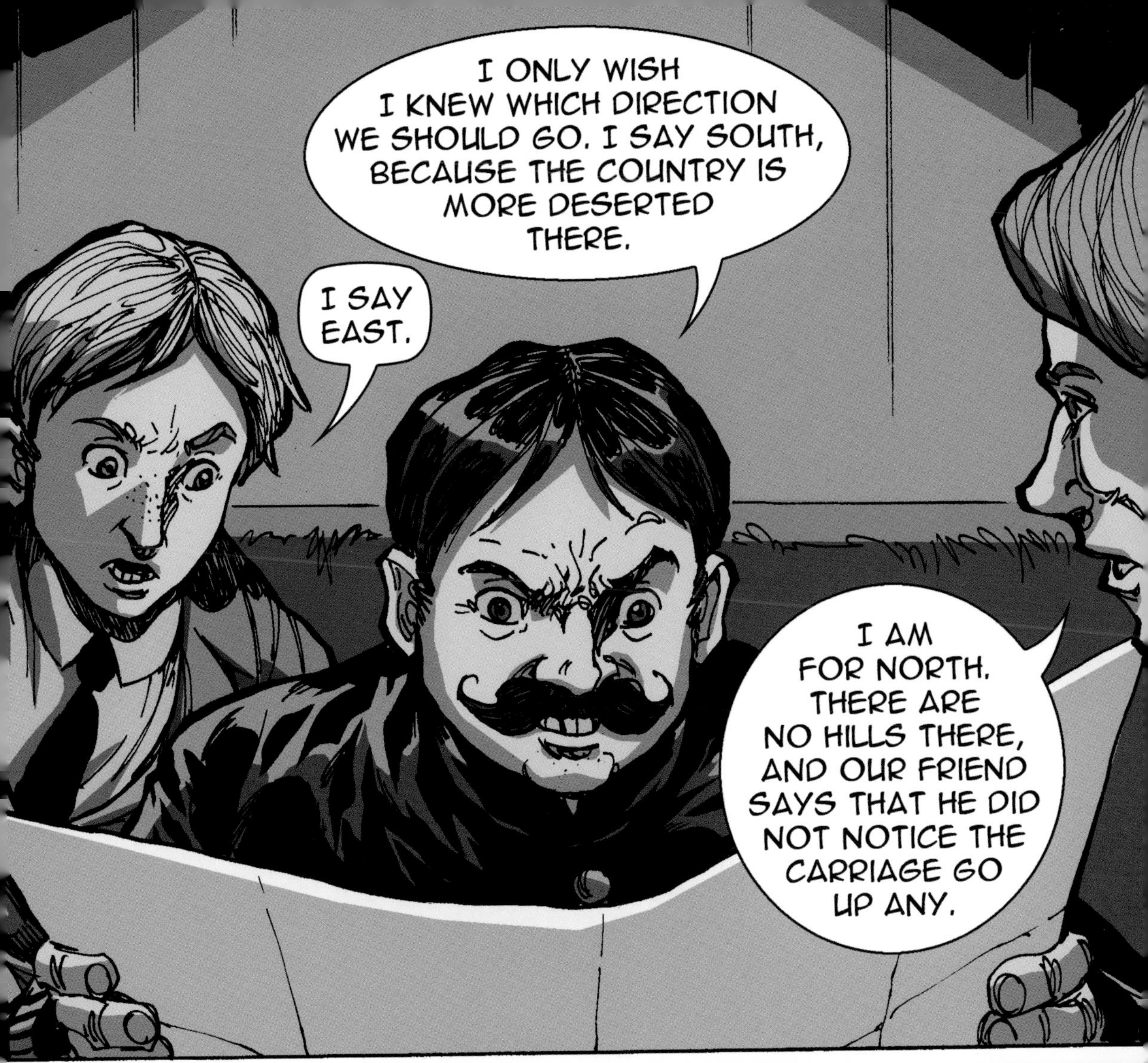
I ONLY WISH I KNEW WHICH DIRECTION WE SHOULD GO. I SAY SOUTH, BECAUSE THE COUNTRY IS MORE DESERTED THERE.
I SAY EAST.
I AM FOR NORTH. THERE ARE NO HILLS THERE, AND OUR FRIEND SAYS THAT HE DID NOT NOTICE THE CARRIAGE GO UP ANY.

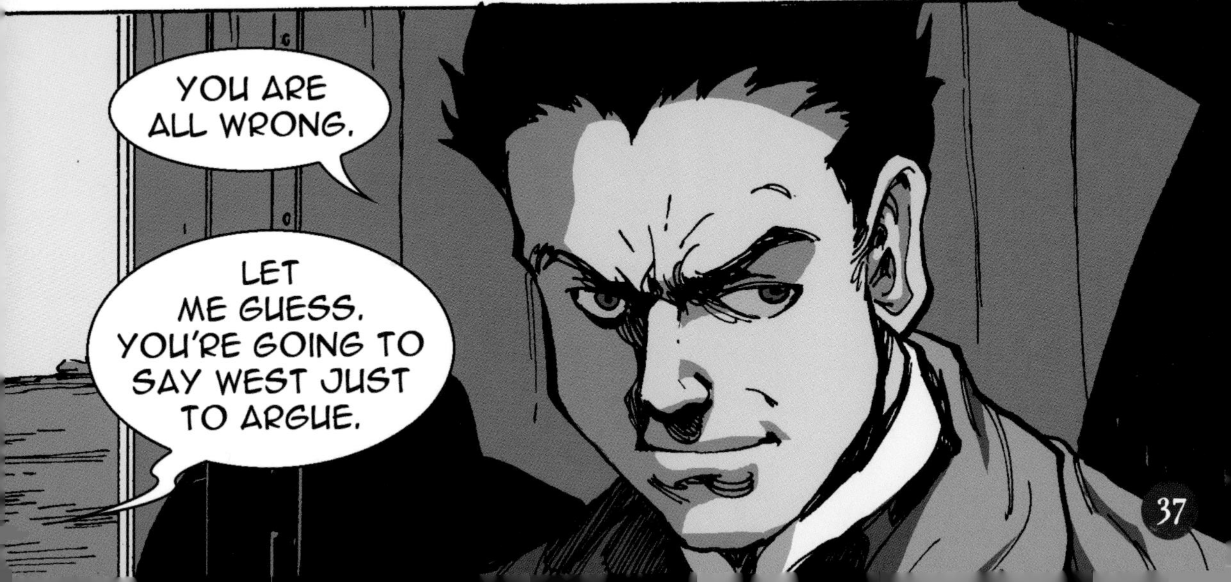
YOU ARE ALL WRONG.
LET ME GUESS. YOU'RE GOING TO SAY WEST JUST TO ARGUE.

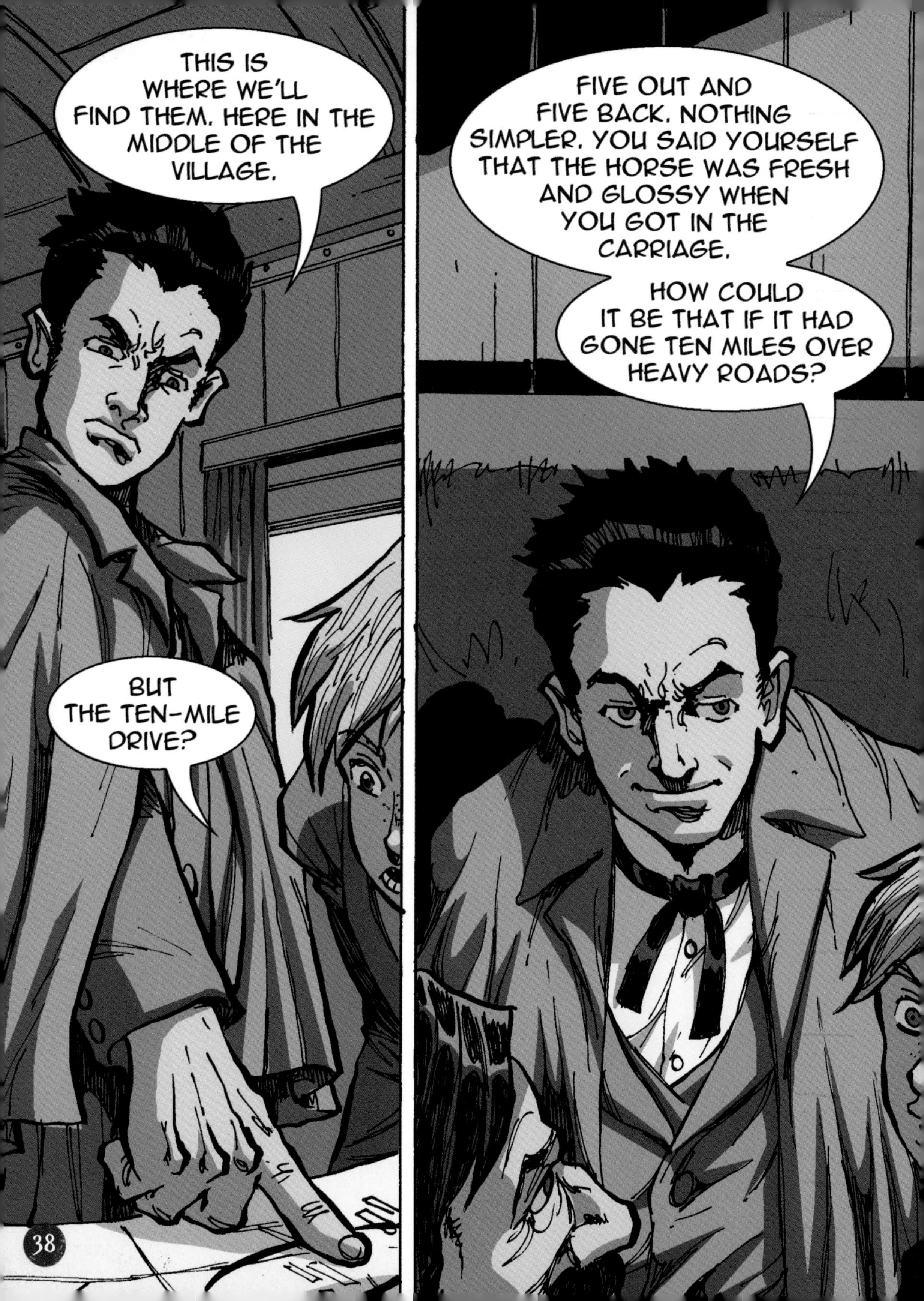
THIS IS WHERE WE'LL FIND THEM. HERE IN THE MIDDLE OF THE VILLAGE.
BUT THE TEN-MILE DRIVE?
FIVE OUT AND FIVE BACK. NOTHING SIMPLER. YOU SAID YOURSELF THAT THE HORSE WAS FRESH AND GLOSSY WHEN YOU GOT IN THE CARRIAGE.
HOW COULD IT BE THAT IF IT HAD GONE TEN MILES OVER HEAVY ROADS?

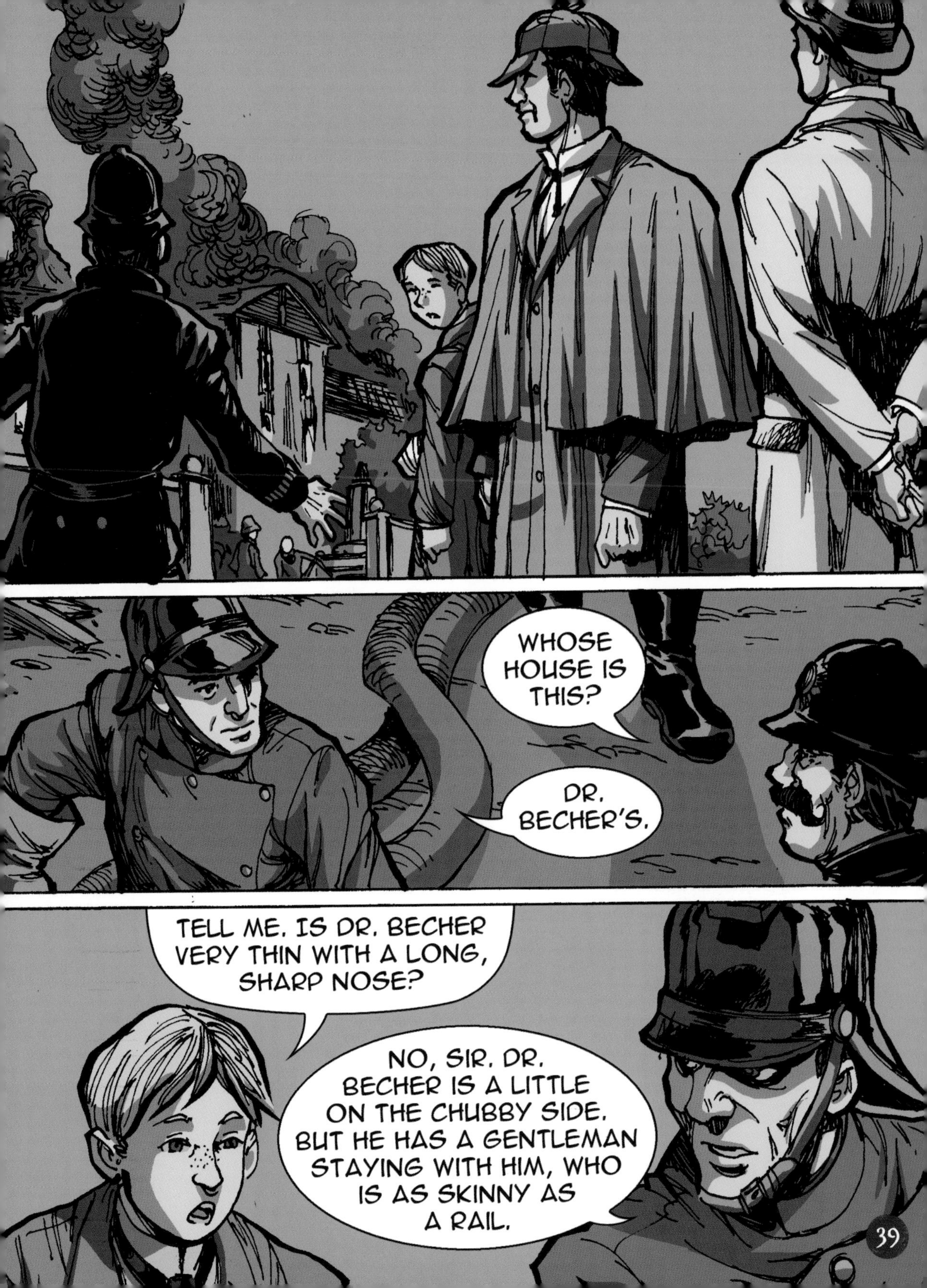
WHOSE HOUSE IS THIS?
DR. BECHER'S.
TELL ME. IS DR. BECHER VERY THIN WITH A LONG, SHARP NOSE?
NO, SIR. DR. BECHER IS A LITTLE ON THE CHUBBY SIDE. BUT HE HAS A GENTLEMAN STAYING WITH HIM, WHO IS AS SKINNY AS A RAIL.

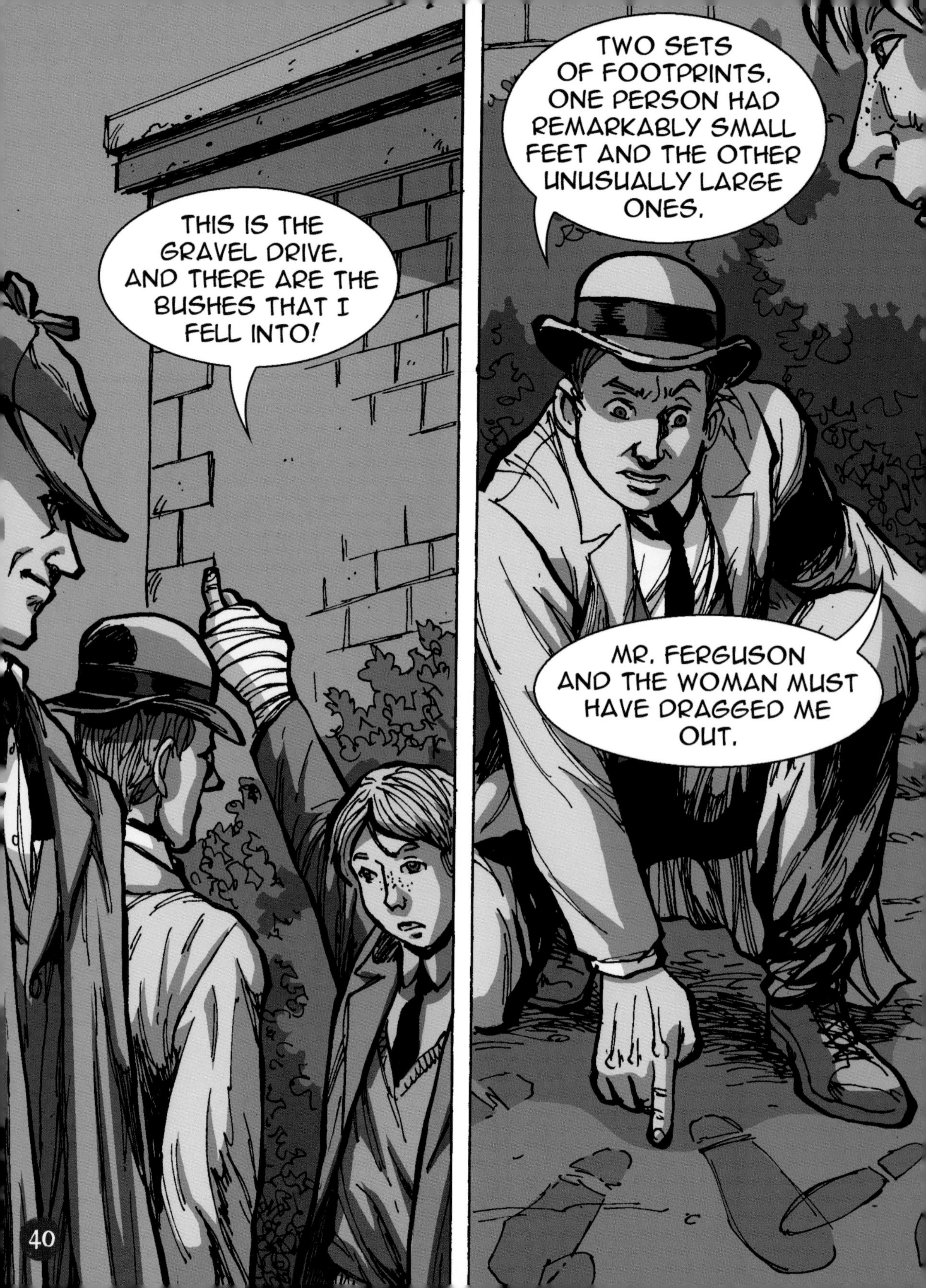
THIS IS THE GRAVEL DRIVE. AND THERE ARE THE BUSHES THAT I FELL INTO!
TWO SETS OF FOOTPRINTS. ONE PERSON HAD REMARKABLY SMALL FEET AND THE OTHER UNUSUALLY LARGE ONES.
MR. FERGUSON AND THE WOMAN MUST HAVE DRAGGED ME OUT.

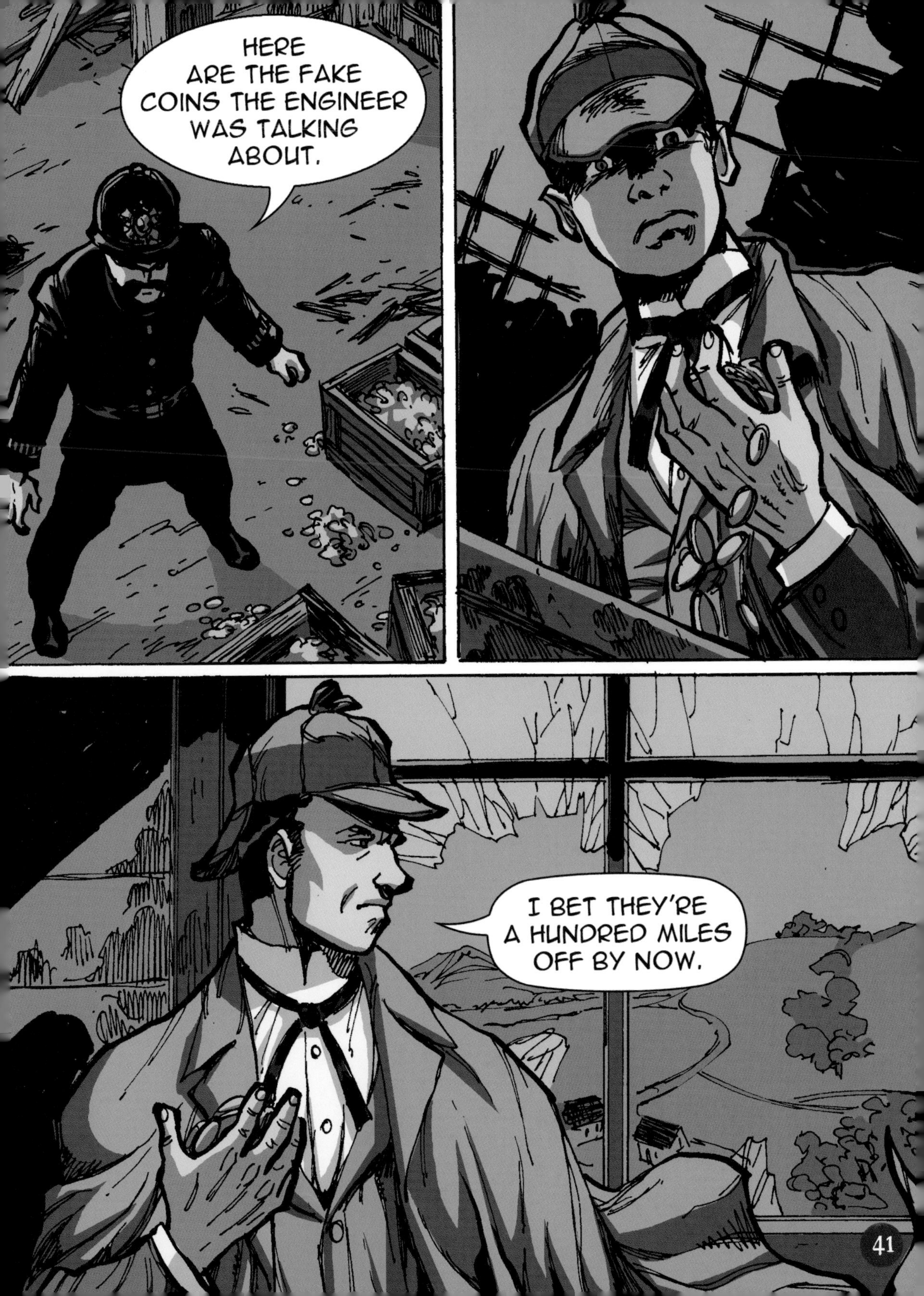
HERE ARE THE FAKE COINS THE ENGINEER WAS TALKING ABOUT.
I BET THEY'RE A HUNDRED MILES OFF BY NOW.

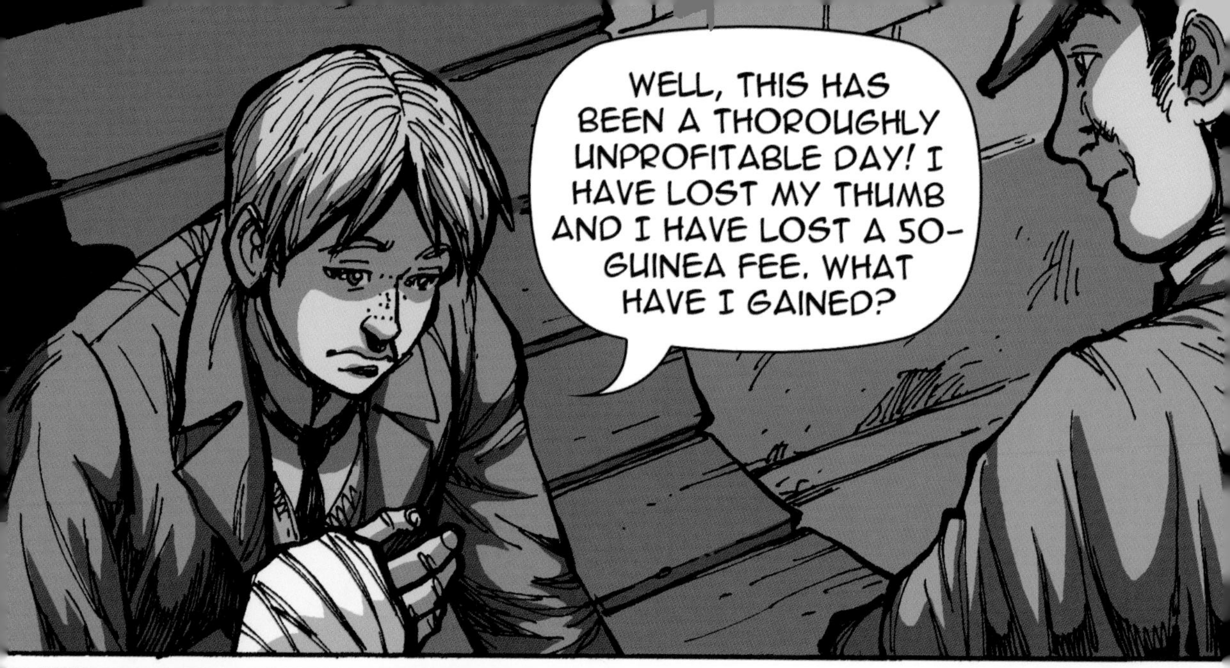
WELL, THIS HAS BEEN A THOROUGHLY UNPROFITABLE DAY! I HAVE LOST MY THUMB AND I HAVE LOST A 50-GUINEA FEE. WHAT HAVE I GAINED?

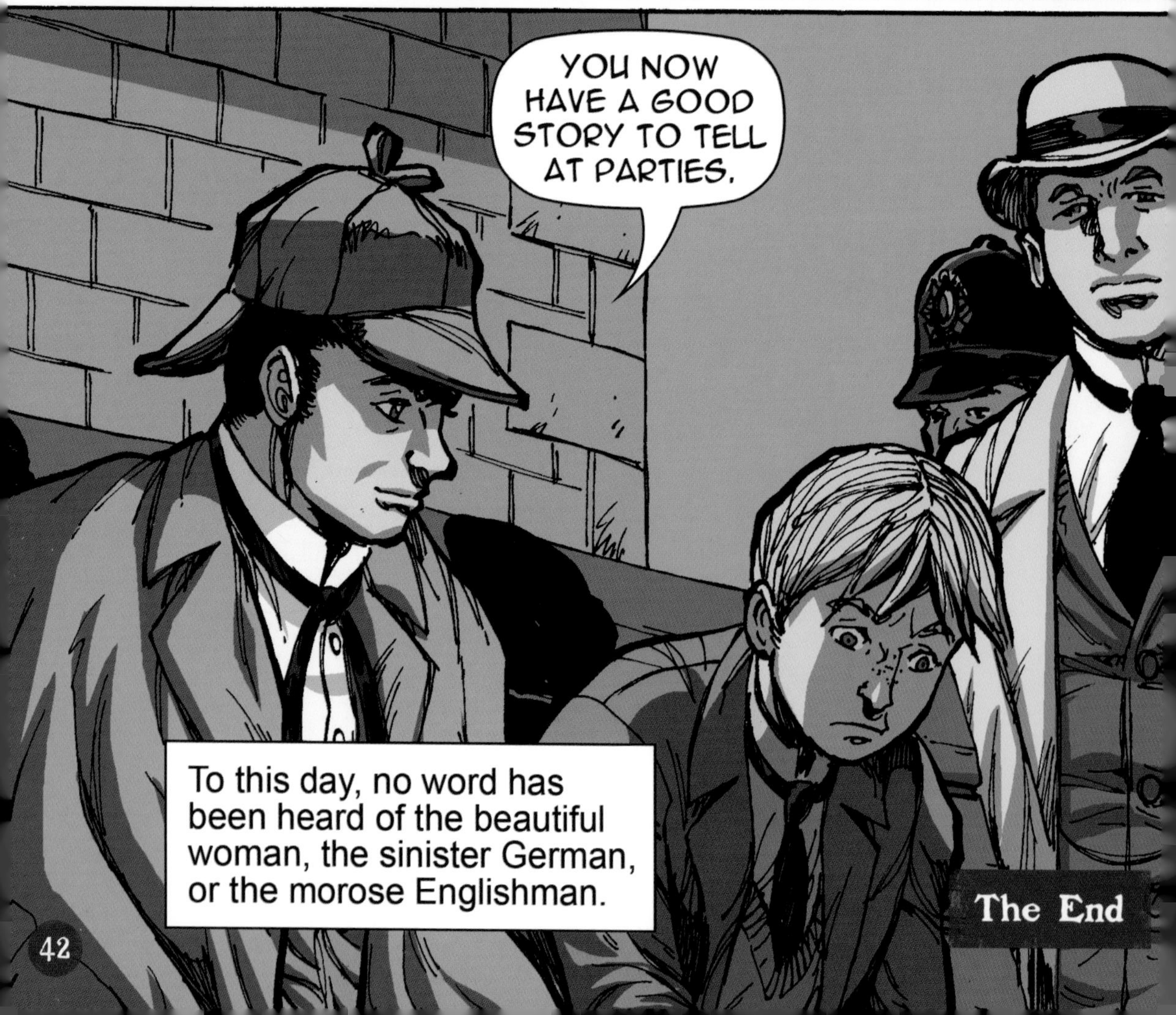
YOU NOW HAVE A GOOD STORY TO TELL AT PARTIES.
To this day, no word has been heard of the beautiful woman, the sinister German, or the morose Englishman.
The End

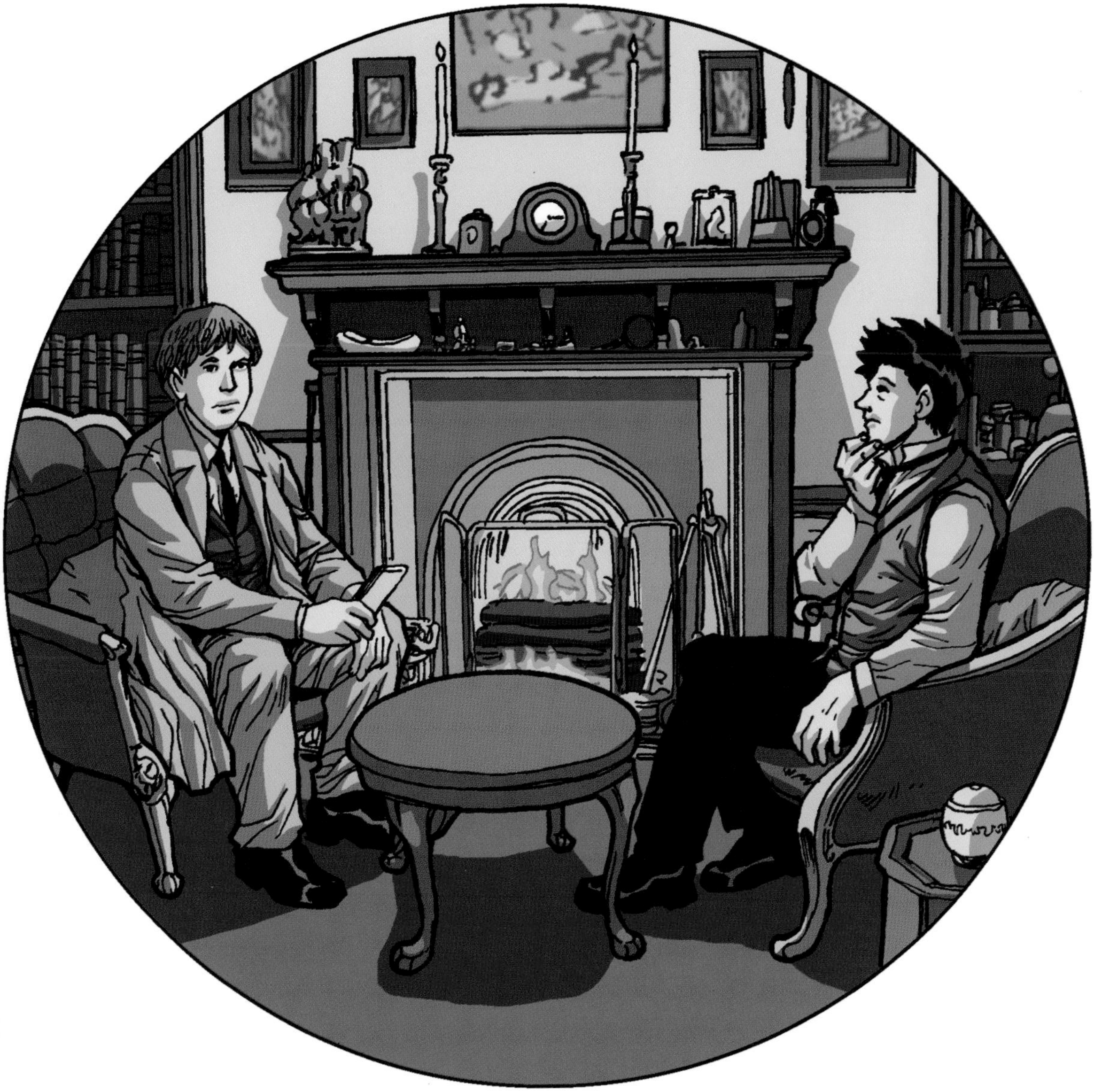

How to Draw
Sherlock Holmes

by Ben Dunn

Step 1: Use a pencil to draw a simple framework. You can start with a stick figure! Then add circles, ovals, and cylinders to get the basic form. Getting the simple shapes in place is the beginning to solving any great case.

Step 2: Time to add to Sherlock's look. Use the shapes you started with to fill in his clothes. Use guidelines to add circles for the eyes. And don't forget the hair.

Step 3: Now you can go in with a pen and start inking Sherlock. Fill in all the details and fix any mistakes. Let the ink dry to avoid smudges, then erase any pencil marks. Sherlock is ready for some color, so grab your markers and get started!

Glossary

accent - a way of speaking a language that is usual for people of a certain area.

bachelor - a man who is not married.

cleaver - a large knife.

convenient - saving work or time; easy.

counterfeit - made to imitate something else in order to deceive.

cylinder - a solid figure of two parallel circles bound by a curved surface. A soda can is an example of a cylinder.

deposit - a collection of mineral matter in nature.

deserted - abandoned.

discreet - done quietly and secretly.

essential - very important or necessary.

excavate - to dig a hole.

force - a push or pull that causes an object to change its speed or the direction it's moving.

forger - someone who falsely makes or alters a document or object, such as a coin.

fuller's earth - earth that has mostly clay minerals and is used to absorb.

guineas - coins used in the United Kingdom.

hydraulic - operated or moved by liquid.

morose - gloomy or angry.

overhaul - to repair thoroughly.

piston - a cylinder fit inside a hollow cylinder in which it moves back and forth. It is moved by or against fluid pressure in an engine.

radius - the area within a circle of a certain size.

reference - a statement of the qualifications of a person for a certain job given by someone who knows them.

secrecy - the condition of being hidden.

sinister - a person or thing that looks dangerous or evil.

socket - an opening that forms a holder for something.

transmit - to send or convey from one person or place to another.

unconscious - not being awake or aware of one's surroundings.

unprofitable - making no money.

utmost - greatest.

Web Sites

To learn more about Sir Arthur Conan Doyle, visit ABDO Group online at **www.abdopublishing.com**. Web sites about Doyle are featured on our Book Links page. These links are routinely monitored and updated to provide the most current information available.

About the Author

Arthur Conan Doyle was born on May 22, 1859, in Edinburgh, Scotland. He was the second of Charles Altamont and Mary Foley Doyle's ten children. In 1868, Doyle began his schooling in England. Eight years later, he returned to Scotland.

Upon his return, Doyle entered the University of Edinburgh's medical school, where he became a doctor in 1885. That year, he married Louisa Hawkins. Together they had two children.

While a medical student, Doyle was impressed when his professor observed the tiniest details of a patient's condition. Doyle later wrote stories where his most famous character, Sherlock Holmes, used this same technique to solve mysteries. Holmes first appeared in *A Study in Scarlet* in 1887 and was immediately popular.

Between 1887 and 1927, Doyle wrote 66 stories and 3 novels about Holmes. He also wrote other fiction and nonfiction novels throughout his life. In 1902, Doyle was knighted for his work in a field hospital in the South African War. Four years later, Louisa died. Doyle married Jean Leckie in 1907, and they had three children together.

Sir Arthur Conan Doyle died on July 7, 1930, in Sussex, England. Today, Doyle's famous character, Sherlock Holmes, is honored with societies around the world that pay tribute to the detective.

Additional Works

A Study in Scarlet (1887)

The Mystery of Cloomber (1889)

The Firm of Girdlestone (1890)

The White Company (1891)

The Adventures of Sherlock Holmes (1891-92)

The Memoirs of Sherlock Holmes (1892-93)

Round the Red Lamp (1894)

The Stark Munro Letters (1895)

The Great Boer War (1900)

The Hound of the Baskervilles (1901-02)

The Return of Sherlock Holmes (1903-04)

Through the Magic Door (1907)

The Crime of the Congo (1909)

The Coming of the Fairies (1922)

Memories and Adventures (1924)

The Case-Book of Sherlock Holmes (1921-27)

About the Adapters

Author

Vincent Goodwin earned his BA in Drama and Communications from Trinity University in San Antonio. He is the writer of three plays as well as the cowriter of the comic book *Pirates vs. Ninjas II*. Goodwin is also an accomplished journalist, having won several awards for his work as a columnist and reporter.

Illustrator

Ben Dunn founded Antarctic Press, one of the largest comic companies in the United States. His works appear in Marvel and Image comics. He is best known for his series *Ninja High School* and *Warrior Nun Areala*.